KINGS OF MAFIA

DRAWN TO DARKNESS

USA TODAY BESTSELLING AUTHOR
MICHELLE HEARD

Copyright © 2024 *DRAWN TO DARKNESS* by M.A. Heard.

All rights reserved. No part of this publication may be reproduced, distributed, or transmitted in any form or by any means, including photocopying, recording, or other electronic or mechanical methods, without the prior written consent of the publisher, except in the case of brief quotation embodied in critical reviews and various other noncommercial uses permitted by copyright law.

The resemblance to actual persons, things, living or dead, locales, or events is entirely coincidental.

Cover Designer: Okay Creations

Editor: Sheena Taylor

TABLE OF CONTENTS

Dedication

Songlist

Synopsis

Drawn To Darkness

Chapter 1

Chapter 2

Chapter 3

Chapter 4

Chapter 5

Chapter 6

Chapter 7

Chapter 8

Chapter 9

Chapter 10

Chapter 11

Chapter 12

Chapter 13

Chapter 14

Chapter 15

Chapter 16

Chapter 17

Chapter 18

Chapter 19

Chapter 20

Chapter 21

Chapter 22

Chapter 23

Chapter 24

Chapter 25

Chapter 26

Chapter 27

Chapter 28

Chapter 29

Chapter 30

Chapter 31

Chapter 32

Chapter 33

Chapter 34

Chapter 35

Chapter 36

Chapter 37

Chapter 38

Epilogue

Published Books

Connect with me

Acknowledgments

Dedication

To Sherrie,

You're one of the strongest people I know. Your cheerfulness and strength inspire me every day.

Songlist

Click here - *Spotify*

Pompeii MMXXIII – Bastille, Hans Zimmer

Into The Fire – Erin McCarley

I Was Here – Beyonce

I'm Not Afraid – Tommee Profitt, Wondra

Helium – Sia

You're Still You – Josh Groban

Alive – Sia

Remember When It Rained – Josh Groban

Angel By The Wings – Sia

You Say – Loren Allred

Light Me Up – Ingrid Michaelson

Never Let Me Go – Florence + The Machine

When You Say You Love Me – Josh Groban

Never Enough – Loren Allred

Synopsis

Poverty is an understatement when it comes to describing my circumstances. My mother is a lost cause I can't get rid of, and I work my fingers to the bone just trying to keep my head above water.

To ease the stress bearing down on my shoulders, I like to dance. Working as a janitor at a ballet company makes it easy for me to steal thirty minutes at night when the place is empty.

Or so I thought. Just my luck that the dangerously handsome owner catches me red-handed. He thinks I'm a hardworking ballerina, and I don't bother correcting him... because, you know, I'd like to keep my job.

Dario La Rosa has every girl at the company swooning, hoping she'll be the one to end his bachelor status. Me? I just want to keep my secret and try to avoid the man at all costs.

But then my mother's sins burst through my dilapidated front door, and my life takes a turn for the worse.

Turns out Dario isn't who I thought he was, and the man has the power to not only change my entire life, but to keep me from losing it.

Even though I'm drawn to the darkness coming off him waves, I'm not sure whether I should run or stay.

What would you do?

Drawn To Darkness

Mafia / Organized Crime / Suspense Romance
STANDALONE in the KINGS OF MAFIA Book 4

Authors Note:
This book contains subject matter that may be sensitive for some readers.
There is triggering content related to:
Graphic violence
Kidnapping
Substance abuse (not main characters)

This book is on the sweeter, more romantic side, so we can catch a breather between Renzo & Damiano.

18+ only.
Please read responsibly.

*"Let us read, and let us dance;
these two amusements will never do any harm to the world."*

—— **Voltaire**

Chapter 1

Eden

Dario La Rosa; 31. Eden Taylor; 24.

Opening my eyes, I listen to the sirens blaring around the neighborhood. It's something you get used to when you live in Brownsville. It's one of The Bronx's poorest and most dangerous areas, but I've learned to navigate the streets.

Sadly, it's home.

The air is stuffy with the early autumn heat, and it has me kicking the covers off.

The AC must be broken again.

I have to talk to the building manager about the faulty heating and broken AC which is a conversation I never look forward to having.

I have to make a plan to buy another blanket, seeing as winter is only a couple of months away, and having heat in this apartment is never a sure thing.

I also have to talk to Sylvia about working extra shifts so I can pay the overdue gas bill.

God. Rent was due last week.

Letting out an exhausted sigh, I drag myself out of bed.

Digging clothes from the drawers of the dresser, I walk to the bathroom and turn on the faucets in the shower. While brushing my teeth, I pray the water will warm up, but when I hold my hand beneath the spray, there's no luck.

I'll have to ask Sylvia for an advance, or it'll be me and cold showers for the next two weeks.

Taking off my underwear and favorite sleepshirt, I step beneath the cold spray and shiver as I rush to wash my hair and body. I keep hopping from one foot to the other as if it will help to warm me up, and the instant I'm done, I dart out of the icy shower.

I grab a bleached towel and dry myself at the speed of light before throwing on my jeans and T-shirt.

"Jesus." I shudder from the cold, and rushing back to my bedroom, I put on my socks and boots.

When I'm fully dressed, I hurry to the kitchen to see if I have any coffee left. Not finding any, I open the fridge and take a sip of the last of the orange juice.

Wanting to avoid Winston, the building manager, until I have the money for rent, I open the window in the small living room and step out onto the steel grate to go down the fire escape.

Just as I head down the stairs, my neighbor, Tyrone, opens his window and pokes his head outside.

"Don't run off. Your mother is passed out in the hallway."

I shake my head and continue down the stairs as I answer, "Not my problem, Tyrone."

"She's your mother," he shouts. "She stinks like the dead."

"Just because the woman gave birth to me doesn't mean shit. Let her sleep in the hallway until Winston throws her out."

When I reach the alley, I glance up to see Tyrone shake his head before shutting his window.

Mandy, the woman who brought me into this world, has never been a mother to me. When I was younger, Tyrone always made sure I had something to eat while Mandy was out getting drunk or high.

The woman doesn't have a motherly bone in her body and is nothing but a thorn in my side. I had to put extra locks on the front door to keep her out. She keeps breaking in and stealing my shit so she can pay for her next hit or her tab at the bar.

Crossing my arms over my chest, I shake my head while I walk to Ben's Burgers, the diner that's responsible for my second income. I always work the twelve to seven shift before heading over to the ballet company, where I work the night shift as a janitor.

If I'm lucky, Sylvia will let me work the morning shift as well.

Who needs sleep when they have bills to pay?

When I reach the diner, it's to see the place is busier than usual.

The second Sylvia lays eyes on me from where she's pinning orders up so Jaden, the cook, will see them, she orders, "Take care of Destiny's section as well as your own. She's not in today."

"Okay," I answer while I quickly walk to the back so I can stash my handbag in my locker. Grabbing my apron, I tie it around my waist before digging my notepad and pencil out.

I get to work, and for the next couple of hours, the place is a madhouse. The sounds of dishes clattering, burger patties sizzling, and orders being given and taken fill the air, along with the smell of old cooking oil.

I don't know why I bother showering before coming in for my shift because I always leave feeling sticky all over.

As soon as there's a lull between customers, I walk to the counter with an apprehensive smile.

Sylvia's eyes flick at me, and with a frown, she says, "What do you want, Eden? If it's time off, you can forget about it. We're already short-staffed."

"Then you'll be happy to hear I need to work an extra shift in the morning."

Keeping her attention on the cash she's taking out of the register so she can put it in the safe, she asks, "For how long?"

"Permanently if possible."

Her gaze darts to me, and I see a rare flicker of concern. "You work nights over at that dance place and afternoons here. When do you plan to sleep?"

I widen my smile and lift my chin. "Sleep is for the dead."

She stares at me for what feels like a solid minute before she says, "I'll let you work half the morning shift."

"But –"

She shakes her head firmly. "Only from nine to twelve. I don't need you dropping dead in my diner."

It's better than nothing.

A group of construction guys comes in, and knowing I have to get back to work, I swallow my pride and ask, "Can I get an advance for the next two weeks?"

Sylvia's eyes narrow on me, which has me adding, "Please. You know I'm good for it."

"I'm not a bank," she mutters as she takes the amount I need from the stack of bills in her hand.

I feel a flicker of relief, but it passes quickly because it's only a temporary fix. At the end of the day, I'm still dead-ass broke, and no matter how hard I work, I can't drag myself out of the poverty I was born into.

When Sylvia hands me the cash, I give her a grateful smile. "Thanks."

She gestures with a nod of her head to the booths and tables. "Get back to work."

I tuck the money into my apron's pocket, and while I take orders, I do the math and hope paying half of the gas bill will have them turning it back on.

At least I can pay Winston the overdue rent.

Just before my shift ends, I find a fifty-dollar tip at one of my tables. I do a little happy dance because it means I can buy coffee and the extra blanket I'll need for winter and put the rest toward the gas bill.

I try to remember who was sitting at the table, but I've served so many people today I give up and decide just to be thankful for the customer's kindness.

When I push the cleaning cart into the restrooms near the studios, a couple of dancers linger in front of the mirror.

After applying a fresh coat of lipstick, the one nearest to the door says, "I saw Madame Stafford and Mr. La Rosa heading toward her office earlier." She wags her eyebrows at her friends. "He is H.O.T."

Moving to the first stall, I get to work and scrub the toilet, not paying much attention to their conversation.

"You can say that again," another girl sighs.

"I didn't see a wedding ring on his finger, so he's still fair game," Lipstick girl says.

Her friend shakes her head while scoffing, "The man is filthy rich. What makes you think he'll give any of us a second glance? He can pick any woman in the country. Besides, if it hasn't happened by now, it will never happen."

Lipstick girl waves her hand over her well-toned body. "No man has ever said no to all of this. I just need an opportunity to get his attention."

Her friend shakes her head again, and when I flush the toilet after scrubbing it, she shoots an uninterested glance my way before saying, "Let's go."

The dancers leave the restroom, and I continue working while I think about the new owner of the ballet company. The name was changed to La Rosa Opera Ballet a while back, and every ballerina I've encountered practically drools over the new owner, whom I haven't seen yet.

Hey, whatever rocks their boat.

When I'm finished with the stalls, I quickly wipe down the sinks before mopping the floor. Pushing my cart out of the restroom, I head down the hallway, glancing into all the studios. Sure everyone has left for the day, I go to where my locker is and change into tight-fitting shorts and a cropped t-shirt.

Every night when the place has emptied out, I steal thirty minutes to dance. It helps ease my stress.

Ever since I was little, I've always loved dancing. I used to put on silly shows for Tyrone, and he used to clap his hands as if he'd witnessed the most epic performance.

A smile tugs around my mouth as I walk to the nearest studio.

Tyrone is a saint. I don't know what I would've done if I didn't have him as a neighbor.

In the studio, I connect my cell phone to the speakers so I can listen to my personal playlist while I dance.

As *Alive* by *Sia* starts to fill the air, I walk to the mirror and lock eyes with my reflection.

Deep breath in...and out.

I'm in control of my life.

Good things will come to me.

I choose to let go of the bad and invite only positive things into my life.

Nodding at myself, I suck in another deep breath before I begin to move. All the stress and worried thoughts fade to the background, and my body takes over.

My heart beats faster and faster, and my breaths speed up as the song's tempo grows. I spin and shoot across the floor, and at times, it feels like I'm flying.

For a blessed moment, I feel free from the suffocating constraints of my life.

As Sia's voice cracks on the high notes, I come to a stop and with my eyes closed, I listen as the song ends.

I take deep breaths of air and slowly lift my lashes.

My playlist skips to the next song, and as *I'm Not Afraid* by *Tommee Profitt* and *Wondra* begins to play, my eyes lock on a man.

Shit.

My chest heaves from all the exercise, and my hands fist at my sides as the shock of seeing the most attractive man I've ever crossed paths with stuns me.

He's leaning with his shoulder against the doorjamb, and even though I don't know much about luxury brands, I'm willing to bet the fifty-dollar tip I got today that the suit he's wearing costs more than I make in a year.

His light brown hair is tousled, which is in total contrast with his expensive clothes, and his brown eyes have a gleam to them I can't quite place. He's taller than the average guy and looks well-built.

As my eyes lock on his face again, I find myself staring once more. There's just something about him that draws me in.

The corner of his mouth lifts while he tilts his head slightly.

The man seems amused by my reaction to him.

Knowing I shouldn't be in the studio, I quickly come to my senses and walk to where I left my phone. I stop the playlist and disconnect my phone before walking to the door, where the man is still leaning against the doorjamb.

When I stop a few steps away from him, I ask, "Can you move so I can pass?"

Instead of doing as I ask, he says, "I was under the impression the place closes at nine."

"Ah...yeah." My tongue darts out to wet my lips. "I was just finishing up."

I'm caught off guard when he holds his hand out to me. "I'm Dario."

Not wanting to be rude, I place my hand in his. There's an instant spark up my arm that ricochets through my body like a lightning bolt.

Damn, this man is all kinds of fine.

As we shake, he says, "Dario La Rosa."

Holleeeeey shit.

The shock hits me square in the chest, and my eyes widen while I quickly rip my hand from his grip.

La Rosa. As in the owner. My bosses' bosses' boss.

I let out a nervous burst of laughter, which is something I always do when I find myself in deep shit.

I begin to squeeze past him so I can make a quick escape while saying, "Gotta run. I have somewhere to be."

At work, cleaning your company.

I'm hit with a whiff of his intoxicating cologne and wouldn't mind another hit, but too scared I'll be caught slacking on the job, I hurry down the hallway.

"You didn't tell me your name," he calls out while chuckling.

"I know," I reply before disappearing around a corner.

Scared he'll come after me, I break out into a run and don't stop until I reach the lockers. I quickly change back into my jeans and t-shirt before dragging on the dark blue cobbler apron. Tying my hair in a ponytail, I put on a company cap.

I wait another ten minutes, and hopeful that Mr. La Rosa has left, I push my cart into the hallway and get back to work.

That was way too close. I'll have to be more careful because if Mr. La Rosa catches me dancing on the job, he'll probably fire me, and I can't afford to lose the income.

Chapter 2

Dario

(3 months later…)

Life has been so fucking busy the past few months I've lost track of time.

I've been helping Renzo with some shit and neglected my own businesses.

Renzo's one of the five heads of the Cosa Nostra, and over the past few months, we've grown closer. My friend kidnapped the best chef in the Northern Hemisphere, and somehow, Skylar fell in love with him.

Lucky bastard.

I'm not going to lie. When he first brought her to his place, I had feelings for the woman, but when I saw them fall in love with each other, I let that shit go. Now I view her the same as the other wives.

Christ. Out of the five of us, only Damiano and I haven't bitten the bullet. Angelo and Franco are fathers and happily married, and I'll bet every last dime to my name

Renzo will have a ring on Skylar's finger before the end of the year.

Damiano will probably never marry. If he does, I pity the woman he chooses. He's the *capo dei capi* – the boss of bosses, and I swear the man's blood runs cold in his veins. I've tried to form a deeper friendship with him, but only Angelo's managed to break through Damiano's hard-as-steel exterior.

Unlike the other four capos, I don't surround myself with soldiers. I prefer to work alone. Then again, I don't need an army of guards because my primary source of income comes from hacking and finding out information no one else can.

The capo title is something I've inherited from my father. I mentioned to the other four to vote someone else into my place, but they didn't want to hear about it.

Besides the ballet company, I also own an opera house. That's where my true passion lies.

Honestly, if I hadn't been born into this position of power, I wouldn't be in the mafia. Where Angelo, Franco, and Renzo trade in illegal arms and counterfeit goods, Damiano makes his fortune from extortion, property control, and construction.

Sure, I can fight, and I'm one of the best snipers, but I'd rather make love than war. It takes a lot to get me upset, and I'm probably the most patient and understanding out of the five of us.

With things calming down a little and Renzo no longer taking up so much of my time, I'm finally able to visit the ballet company. I was hoping to get here earlier, but I got held up at the opera house.

As I near the first studio, my eyes scan over all the dancers. I've always loved fine art, plays, and opera shows. When I discovered the ballet company was on the market, I didn't waste any time purchasing it.

There's just something magical about this world.

I watch as the women practice, their graceful movements in perfect sync. One of the ballerinas notices me, and she stumbles over her feet, earning her a stern scolding from the teacher.

I move on to the next studio, where three women have just finished with a session. This time, I'm spotted instantly, and before I can make my escape, they come rushing toward me.

One of the dancers breaks away and holds her hand out to me. "Mr. La Rosa! I'm Phoebe. It's such an honor meeting you in person."

"Nice to meet you," I murmur.

I shake her hand, and as I pull away, she brushes her palm over my bicep, looking up at me with blatant interest.

For a moment, I contemplate asking her to join me for dinner, but then a certain woman pops into my mind. I've only seen the dancer once, and she was nothing like the perfect ballerina in front of me. Quite the opposite.

The woman I saw a while back had wild black hair, and she danced with so much passion it instantly gripped my attention. Her movements weren't perfect, which only lent to her wild persona.

"Would you…" Phoebe starts to say something.

I cut her off with a curt, dismissive nod while murmuring, "Ladies."

Walking away, I glance into the other studios, and when I don't see the mysterious dancer, I feel disappointed. It would be a pity if she no longer danced at my company.

I head to Mrs. Stafford's office. The dancers call her Madame Stafford, and she's responsible for running the company.

When I step into her office, a welcoming smile curves her lips as she says, "It's been a while since you graced us with your presence."

I take a seat opposite her desk. "I've been busy."

She presses a button on her desk phone. When her receptionist answers, she orders, "Please bring two cups of tea."

She leans back in her chair, and her eyes sweep over my face. "Are you just visiting, or is there something I can help with?"

"Just visiting. How's the preparation for the winter show coming along?"

"Very good," she replies. "We have three ladies who shine above the rest."

Probably the dancers I just met.

The office door opens, and Astrid brings in a tray of tea. After she sets it down on the desk, she leaves, and I wait for Mrs. Stafford to hand me a cup before I ask, "Do you know all the dancers?"

She nods while taking a sip of her beverage. "As you're aware, every applicant has to audition before they're permitted to join the company."

"I ran into a dancer a while back. She's a head and a half shorter than me and has curly black hair that reaches past her shoulders. Gray eyes," I say, hating that I don't have a better description of the woman.

Mrs. Stafford lets out a contained burst of laughter. "Half our dancers have black hair." She glances at the diamond-encrusted wristwatch, then mentions, "The rehearsal is about to start. Will you be joining me?"

Finishing the tea, I set the cup down as I rise to my feet. "Of course."

Leaving the office we make our way to the auditorium where the rehearsal has just begun. I take a seat in the middle of all the rows, and soon, I'm absorbed by the graceful movements of the ballerinas.

When the performance ends two hours later, I remain seated while the auditorium clears out. Silence wraps around me as I soak in the ambience left behind by the dancers.

My phone vibrates in my pocket, and pulling it out, I see a notification from the facial recognition program I have running at home. I've been searching for Servando Montes, a dead-man-walking, who's at the top of Renzo's list of enemies.

The match is only partial, and after checking the photo of a man at a gas station, I delete the notification and pocket my cell phone again.

I've been getting a ton of partial matches, and a few weeks ago, I almost tracked down Montes in Europe. I'm tired of the cat-and-mouse game and wish the fucker would crawl out of whatever hole he's hiding in so we can put an end to this shit.

The lights turn off, filling the auditorium with darkness, and it has me digging my phone out of my pocket again. Checking the time, I see it's already past nine.

I suppose I better go home and get back to work.

Letting out a sigh, I get up from the seat I'm occupying and use the flashlight on my phone as I make my way to one of the exits.

The place is empty as I walk toward the section where the studios are, but as I turn up the hallway, I hear music playing.

The corner of my mouth lifts, and when I reach the open door of the studio, the lyrics, '*I was here,*' fill the air as the elusive dancer I was asking Mrs. Stafford about does a double twirl before leaping through the air.

My heartbeat speeds up as I watch the mistake-riddled dance unfold before me, and a sense of calm I'd pay millions for pours through my body.

The woman must be a beginner because her movements lack grace and years of training, but still, I can't tear my eyes away from her.

Unlike most ballerinas, her skin is tanned, and her black hair isn't tied back in a tight bun. She's wearing a mismatched outfit, and her feet are bare.

She's the complete opposite of the ballerinas who work themselves to the bone to achieve perfection.

My eyes rove over her tanned skin, glistening with a layer of sweat, and the sight makes lust unfurl in my chest.

The first time I saw her and we had the short interaction, I felt the attraction between us. Where I felt protective of Skylar when we met, I want to throw this woman down on the floor so I can rip the tight shorts and flimsy shirt off her body.

There's an urge to see if she's strong enough to handle a rough fuck.

My phone begins to vibrate, and with a frown forming on my forehead, I pull the device out.

Seeing Renzo's name on the screen, I answer, "What's up?"

The black-haired beauty's eyes lock on me, and even though surprise flashes over her features, she continues to dance.

"Nothing," he replies. "Just wanted to check in with you."

My gaze remains glued to the woman as she runs toward me, and a couple of steps away, she suddenly stops before moving backward while her arms appear to be reaching for me.

Jesus. Fucking. Christ.

I have to suppress the urge to grab hold of her and blink like a lust-struck idiot while I mutter, "No news yet. The moment the fucker pops up, you'll be the first to know."

"Am I interrupting something?" he asks.

"No. I'm watching one of the ballerinas."

I hear laughter in his tone as he asks, "Watching or stalking?"

My eyes narrow on the beauty as she leaps into the air. "Both."

Renzo chuckles before teasing me by saying, "You gonna be her mystery man?"

"Nope, that's Franco's title." We give Franco endless shit about the name Samantha, his wife, gave him.

One song blends into another, and when my dancer doesn't stop, it fills me with satisfaction.

"She knows I'm watching, and I think she loves it," I tell my friend.

"Hmm…sounds like you have the hots for her," Renzo continues to tease me.

If hots equate to lust and wanting to have her legs wrapped around me, then yes.

"Watching her dance calms me," I admit in a low tone.

"You can do with some calmness in your life. I'll talk to you later. Enjoy the show."

"I will," I chuckle before ending the call and focusing all my attention on the dancer.

Chapter 3

Eden

I'm playing with fire, and while self-preservation screams for me to get out of the studio and back to work, I don't stop because the way Mr. La Rosa looks at me makes me feel hot and bothered.

An intense sexual tension keeps building between us until I'm contemplating throwing caution to the wind and flirting with the man.

Maybe I could risk a one-night stand with him?

Nope. Not risking my job.

Breaking out of the trance the man has me in, I stop dancing and head to the table where my phone is. I disconnect it from the speakers, and silence falls heavily around me.

I can feel Mr. La Rosa's eyes burning into my back, and it makes the heat in my abdomen increase with intensity.

I suck in a couple of deep breaths before I turn around and walk toward the doorway. He straightens up from where he's leaning against the doorjamb, and a mischievous smile tugs at the corner of his mouth.

"Are you going to tell me your name tonight?" he asks, his voice deep and rough.

Having anonymity on my side, I feel way too brave for my own good.

Stopping inches away from him, I slowly tilt my head back while a seductive smile curls my lips up. "No." The single word is breathless and filled with heat.

Mr. La Rosa's eyes sharpen on my face. "I like a challenge."

I move forward, and as I pass by him, my shoulder brushes against his arm as I say, "Good for you."

As I walk down the hallway, I hear him say, "Same time, same studio, tomorrow night."

"We'll see," I reply.

The instant I disappear around the corner, I lift my hand to my chest and suck in deep breaths.

What the hell am I doing? Risking my job like this is stupid.

Still… Having Mr. La Rosa's attention on me feels too good to resist.

Ugh. Now I'm drooling over him, just like all the other dancers at the company.

Only, I'm not one of his dancers. I'm his janitor.

Reaching my locker, I change out of the shorts and shirt and into my regular clothes and apron. When I've tied my hair and put on the cap with the company logo, I check my cleaning cart while I give Mr. La Rosa some time to leave.

Feeling I need to wait an extra ten minutes, I pull the paper bag with the food I brought from the diner out of the locker.

I'm so tired of diner food, but I have no time to cook and zero money to buy something healthier.

A free meal is a free meal.

I open the container, and taking the plastic fork from the bag, I shovel some spaghetti and meatballs into my mouth.

While I eat, my thoughts revolve around Mr. La Rosa as if it's stuck on spin cycle.

Dario.

I like his name.

And the way the man fills a suit. Yum.

His tousled hair makes my fingers itch to find out if the strands are as thick as they look.

And his eyes. Boy, do those eyes possess a magnetic pull that's hard to resist.

I wonder what his reaction would be if he found out I'm a janitor and not a professional ballerina.

The man is so far out of my league we might as well be from different solar systems.

That fact alone should be enough to deter me from ever crossing paths with him again. Never mind that he's my boss and so high up the food chain, I'm not even privileged enough to eat his scraps.

I use the fork to break a meatball in half and shove a piece into my mouth.

Jaden put too much tomato paste in the sauce again. It's the last time I'm taking the spaghetti and meatballs. The man, who's the only cook at the diner, makes a mean cheese and bacon burger, though, but I can't eat that every day.

Putting the rest of the food away, I drink some water straight from the faucet by the sink before pushing the cleaning cart into the hallway. I mop everywhere, then retrieve the floor polisher from the supply room.

I put my earbuds in and press play on my playlist before I switch the machine on. With the handle vibrating in my grip, my thoughts keep straying, and I find myself thinking way too much of Dario La Rosa.

I'm pretty sure he also feels attracted to me. At least, the version of me he's seen dancing in the studio.

I let out a snort when I think about how quickly he'd lose interest if he had to see me now.

The thought isn't upsetting, because I don't waste time wishing for things I can't have. I focus on my reality, and the fact that I'm able to pay my bills is all that matters.

I might be poor but things can always be worse.

Thinking of worse. I haven't seen Mandy, my birthgiver, in a long while.

My eyebrow lifts for a moment, but I seriously couldn't care less about the woman.

Movement catches my eye, and when I see Mr. La Rosa exiting one of the offices, I frantically glance around for a place to hide.

Not wanting to draw his attention, I duck my head low and hope to all that's holy he doesn't take notice of me.

He walks toward me, but the stars are on my side when he heads up a hallway toward the entrance of the building.

Thank God for small mercies.

Pushing the floor polisher forward, I peek up the other hallway and drink in the sight of Mr. La Rosa's broad shoulders.

Forget about the man, Eden. It's a waste of time.

After my shift at the diner, I open my front door and step inside my apartment. My eyes instantly lock on the busted windowpane that's been jimmied open. A crowbar lies on the floor, and it has anger pouring through me like hot lava.

After a grueling day at work, this is the last thing I have energy for, and I know who the culprit is.

"Mandy," I shout, and not seeing the pain in my ass in the living room or kitchen, I rush in the direction of my bedroom.

I swear, if she's in my bed, I'm going to lose my ever-loving shit.

"Mandy!" Not finding her there, I head to the bathroom, where I find the god-awful woman passed out on the floor with an empty bottle of cheap rum lying beside her.

"Wake up!" I demand while I nudge her stinking ass with the toe of my sneaker. "Mandy. Wake up and get out of my place."

She doesn't budge at all, and not tolerating her for a second longer, I grab hold of her ankles and begin to drag her toward the front door.

"Over my dead body, am I letting you sleep here. I want you gone. Forever," I mutter angrily.

When I lug her unconscious ass out into the hallway, Tyrone opens his door. Seeing my mother, drunk off her ass, he just shakes his head, then says, "I've made pot roast. Want some before you go to your second job?"

I let go of her ankles, and they land with a thud on the floor. Instantly my mood perks up as I jokingly say, "Does a bear shit in the woods?"

He lets out a chuckle then gestures into his apartment.

I shake my head. "She busted my window. I just want to fix it, then I'll be over."

"I'll take a look," Tyrone says. "Let me grab my toolbox."

I give him a wide smile. "You're so good to me."

Stepping over Mandy, I head back inside and pick up the crowbar. Shaking my head, I inspect the damage to the windowpane and wonder how we're going to fix it so Mandy can't get in again.

"I can nail the thing shut," Tyrone suddenly says from behind me. "But you won't be able to use the fire escape to avoid Winston when rent is due."

"It's either that, or I'll have to ask Winston to put in a new window with a lock, which will cost money I don't have. He sure as hell won't pay for it."

I let out a sigh as I watch Tyrone get to work. As long as I've known Tyrone, I've never seen him with a woman. Whenever I ask him why, he just says he doesn't have time for a romantic relationship. It's kind of always been me and him.

He secures the wooden window frame to the windowsill with three long nails, then mutters, "Let's go eat, baby girl."

I wrap my arm around his lower back and give him a sideways hug as we walk out of my apartment. I quickly lock the door behind me and side-sidestepping Mandy, we head to Tyrone's kitchen for a quick bite to eat before I have to leave for my night shift.

When Tyrone pulls a loaded plate of food out of the oven that he was keeping warm for me, there's a swell of emotion in my heart.

I take the plate with a grateful smile, and walking to the small round table, I grab a seat.

Tyrone grabs two beers from the fridge and comes to join me.

"You still working double shifts at the diner?" he asks, even though he already knows the answer.

I enjoy a bite of the pot roast while nodding.

"You're working yourself into the ground," he mutters. "I made some extra money at the last construction job. Let me help you."

"No." I shake my head hard. "I'm not taking your money, Tyrone. You're not doing any better than me."

He gives me a pleading look. "We gotta take care of each other. What will I do if you drop dead from exhaustion?"

"You can take Mandy under your wing," I joke. "She's always hard up for a place to crash."

"Don't even joke about her," he mumbles before taking a sip of beer. "It's a fucking miracle she's still alive."

"She's like a weed. Nothing kills that shit."

He waits for me to help myself to another bite of the healthy and delicious food, then says, "Take the money. It will help me sleep at night because right now, I'm up worrying about your ass."

Giving him a grateful smile, I shake my head again. "You know I can't take your money. Besides, I only have to work a double shift for another three months, then I'll have some savings to fall back on."

"You're so fucking stubborn," he complains.

"Yeah, I know." Letting out a burst of laughter, I add, "You're the one who taught me to be stubborn." I eat for a while, then say, "I want to make Thanksgiving dinner this year."

"I've tasted your cooking, and no offense, but you can't cook for shit."

I shoot a playful glare at Tyrone. "Then teach me instead of complaining."

A smile spreads over his face. "Does that mean you'll take the day off for Thanksgiving? A turkey takes hours to cook?"

"Shoot," I mutter. "I didn't think about that."

Chuckling, he winks at me. "Then it's settled. I'll make Thanksgiving dinner like always."

"Fine," I grumble before finishing the rest of my food. "You win."

I wash the delicious meal down with the beer before I get up to wash the plate and utensils.

"What are you going to do about Mandy?" Tyrone asks from where he's still sitting at the table.

"Nothing. She can lie in the hallway until Winston throws her out."

"I'm not talking about that. She keeps coming back and breaking into your place. You still haven't replaced half the shit she stole the last time she broke in."

I shrug because there's not much I can do besides moving, and I'm not doing that.

"This is the first time we've seen her in months. With a little luck, she'll disappear again."

"You saw the track marks on her arms. What if she owes another dealer money, and they come knocking again? The last time they hurt you."

Yeah, I haven't forgotten. I had a black eye for a week.

"All the dealers around here know I don't have money to pay Mandy's debts," I say, even though I know that won't stop them from busting down my front door.

Damn, I wish the woman would permanently disappear from my life. She's never done anything for me and only brought me pain and worry.

Finished with the dishes, I dry my hands as I glance at Tyrone. "Don't worry. One of these days, she won't bother coming around anymore."

Tyrone lets out a sigh, and when I head for the front door, he says, "Be careful out there."

"I will."

Heading back to my apartment, so I can change into clean clothes for my night shift at the ballet company, I step over Mandy again.

I have to resist the urge not to kick her for all the trouble she keeps causing in my life.

Chapter 4

Dario

Last week, I finally found Servando Montes. I went to Mexico with Renzo, where he killed the fucker. It was a waste of my time because Renzo didn't need me there. Since then, things have been super quiet, and I find myself spending more and more time at the ballet company.

I'm hoping to see my elusive dancer, but there's been no sign of her. I've checked through all the files of the ballerinas, and she's not among them.

I'm thinking she's friends with one of the ballerinas who lets her in so she can dance without paying the fee. I've asked the guard at the front desk, but he has no idea who I'm talking about.

It's frustrating.

Sitting in the empty auditorium, I check my emails and find two requests from clients. One is to hack into a company to steal information, and the other is to track an assassin. I accept the jobs, and hearing movement by one of the side doors, I glance in the direction and see a janitor pushing a cart into the auditorium. When a vacuum cleaner is also brought into the room, I decide to leave before the noise starts.

I walk toward the studios, hoping to see my elusive dancer. I swear, the next time I catch her, I'm not leaving without knowing her name.

As I turn into the hallway, I don't hear any music, and it's soon apparent she's not here.

I let out a disappointed sigh as I walk into the studio she previously used. Grabbing one of the chairs by the side of the wall, I take a seat.

I'm one of the best when it comes to finding someone, and I plan on using my talent to find the woman. I just need to check the surrounding area for CCTV cameras, tap into their feed, and find one of her. After that, a quick facial recognition scan will lead me straight to her.

I decide to wait ten minutes, hoping I won't have to track her down, and sitting in the studio, I catch myself listening for footsteps.

When it's clear she's not coming tonight, I'm about to get up when my attention's drawn by sudden movement.

A smile spreads over my face at the sight of my elusive dancer finally making her appearance.

She doesn't notice me, and I watch as she connects her phone to the speakers. When a song starts, she goes to stand in front of the wall-to-ceiling mirrors that cover the entire wall.

She stares at her reflection for a moment before she starts to move.

I recognize the song because I'm a huge Hans Zimmer fan. It's the one he did with Bastille. I listened to it on an endless loop when it came out.

The woman who's managed to capture and hold my attention moves as if she's a light breeze in an open field.

My phone begins to vibrate, and I quickly decline the call before switching off the device. I want no interruptions. I've waited over a week for this performance.

As the tempo of the song grows in intensity, she claws at the air, her face filled with so much emotion it steals my breath right from my lungs.

Christ, she's fucking breathtakingly beautiful.

A strong emotion creeps into my chest, and I know with dead certainty I want to get to know everything about her.

I want to spend endless hours talking to her.

I want to map her body with my tongue and hands.

I want to fuck her until she's so breathless she's begging for air.

She's in the middle of a twirl when she spots me and almost loses her balance as she comes to a sudden stop.

The previous times, she kept dancing for me, but tonight, she stares at me while her chest heaves with rushed breaths.

Slowly, I climb to my feet, and with every step I take toward the middle of the floor where she's standing, I feel the tension between us build.

When I reach her, she tilts her head back, and with parted lips, she looks at me.

I lift my hand, and getting to brush my fingertips over the curve of her jaw makes a strong current of attraction zap through me.

I see the same desire that's coursing through my veins reflecting in her gray eyes, and it has me lowering my head until I can feel her hot breaths bursting on my lips.

"Where have you been?" I ask, my tone low and demanding.

"Busy," she murmurs as if she's stuck in a trance.

"Hmm…" I lean closer and take a deep breath of her natural scent. "Is this what you'll smell like after I've fucked you?"

The burst of laughter erupting from her is the last reaction I expected to my question. She pulls away, and shaking her head, she says, "Wow. Ahhh…okay."

Walking to where her phone is, she disconnects it and makes a beeline for the door.

I dart after her, and grabbing hold of her bicep, I stop her from running away.

There's a surprised expression on her face when she looks at me again. "I have to go."

Not giving her what she wants, I tug her closer and ask, "What's your name?"

She shakes her head again. "I'm not giving you my name."

Her refusal has heat flooding my veins, and before I can rethink things, I lift my other hand to the back of her neck and slam my mouth down on hers.

If I thought she would try to fight me off, I'm sorely mistaken. My black-haired beauty unleashes a level of passion on me I've never received from a woman, and the kiss goes from unplanned to downright filthy and hungry in a split second.

She kisses the way she dances. It's not perfect, and I can't anticipate her next move because it's wild as fuck.

Her hands come up between us, and while one roams the expanse of my chest, the other one grips my hard as fuck cock through the fabric of my pants. She fucking squeezes until she draws a groan from me, and I can't resist the urge to thrust against her hand.

Christ. I want her so fucking badly.

Usually, at the very least, I know the woman's name before I fuck her, but right now I couldn't care less.

Just as I grab the waistband of her tight-fitting shorts so I can rip them from her body, she pulls away, and before I can draw a desperate breath, she darts out of the studio like a rabbit that's been spooked.

It takes another precious second before I break out into a run to chase after her, and as I explode into the hallway, it's in time to see her disappear around the corner.

I race after the woman who's playing a game I intend to win, but as I reach the corner, the hallway she ran into is empty.

Where the fuck did she go?

Not giving up so easily, I begin to search for her, even going as far as to look in the storage rooms, locker rooms, and restrooms.

When I reach the auditorium, it's with a sinking feeling that I realize she's managed to escape me.

For now.

I swear the next time I lay eyes on her, I'll drag her ass to one of the offices, where I'll lock the door so she can't run.

I hear the sound of the vacuum cleaner coming from the auditorium, and turning around, I head to the exit so I can get my ass home. I'm going to check every CCTV camera in the area. One of them must've caught her, and from there, it will be as easy as taking candy from a kid to track her down.

Chapter 5

Eden

Dear God, what was I thinking?

I wasn't. That's the problem.

Just like the other times I've seen Dario, I was practically mesmerized by the man. The pull coming from him is impossible to ignore.

The moment he touched me, I knew it would be hard to deny him anything, and when he kissed me, I was overcome with searing desire.

Holy shit, was I overcome.

If I'm not careful, I'm going to fall hard and fast for my boss, and that would be disastrous. People like him don't mix with people like me. His kind uses my kind to climb to the top and disposes of us like trash when they're done with us.

Still.

God, when he kissed me. When I felt his rock-hard cock through the luxurious fabric of his pants. The man is packing, and I know it will hurt the first time he's inside me. When I inhaled breath after breath of his addictive scent.

It was all so intoxicating I didn't know whether I was coming or going.

Stop it, Eden!

He almost caught you tonight. You need the money a hell of a lot more than you need a quick fuck that won't mean a thing.

It might turn out to be the best fuck of your life, but it won't pay the bills.

When I went to the studio, I thought he'd already left. I even waited fifteen minutes to make sure it was safe.

I've been trying to avoid him, but at this rate, I'll have to give up my stolen thirty minutes in the studio.

While I continue to vacuum the auditorium, my thoughts turn away from what I'm going to do to avoid Dario to how it felt kissing him.

The firm strokes of his tongue.

Feeling his breath on my lips.

His strong fingers gripping the back of my neck.

His solid body pressed against mine.

His hard cock…

Hot dammmmnnnnnn.

Sucking in a deep breath, I shove the memory down so I can focus on getting my work done, but with the taste of Dario lingering in my mouth, it's impossible.

I should've let him fuck me. At least then I wouldn't feel so needy right now.

I let out a snort and shake my head at myself.

Wiping down a table, I glance through the window at the rain pouring down outside.

The diner is quiet, and when I'm done, I walk to the counter and get myself a cup of coffee.

"Sylvia said we can have yesterday's pie," Sherrie says. "Pour me coffee while I cut two slices for us."

"Okay." I take a seat at the counter, and when Sherrie places the apple pie in front of me, I take a bite.

"So, what's news in your life?" she asks when she comes to sit next to me.

Sherrie and I have worked the longest at Ben's Burgers. She's one of the strongest and most beautiful people I know. Whenever life deals her a blow, she hits back twice as hard.

"Not much." I lick stray crumbs off my lips, then admit, "You know I work the night shift over at La Rosa Opera Ballet, right?"

"Yeah."

"The owner is…" I let out a dreamy sigh, "hot as fuck."

Her eyebrows lift as she gives me a curious look. "Ooooh."

I can't stop from grinning like an idiot when I admit, "We kissed."

Sherrie grabs my forearm as she leans closer for the juicy news. "And? How was it? Are you dating?"

Letting out a chuckle, I reply, "The kiss was amazing, but no, we're not dating. We never will. I'm actually avoiding him."

"Why?" She shakes her head at me. "You should go for it."

I give her an incredulous look. "He's filthy rich, and I'm dirt poor."

"So?"

I let out a sigh as I tear the apple pie apart with my fork. "He's my boss, and I can't risk losing the income."

Her shoulders slump, and reaching for her mug, she mutters, "That sucks."

"Yeah." I eat some more of the pie before asking, "How are things in your life?"

"Much better. Tanner finally pulled his head out of his ass and got a job."

"That's amazing." I give her a happy grin. "I'm glad things are looking up for you."

Someone coming into the diner draws our attention, and when I see it's Mandy, I shoot up from the stool I'm sitting on.

"Get out, Mandy," I order while walking toward her.

"Is that how you treat your mother?" she mutters, not as drunk or high as she usually is.

Her black hair is a ratty mess, and she's filthy. God only knows when she last had a bath.

She slides into a booth, then says, "After all I've done for you."

"You haven't done shit for me," I say with a burst of unbelievable laughter. "Get out. This is my workplace."

She lifts her chin and digs crumbled notes and coins out of her pocket. "I'm a paying customer."

Ugh. This woman is unbearable.

"I'll take her order," Sherrie says.

I shoot a scalding glare at Mandy before I give Sherrie a grateful look. "Thanks. I owe you."

As I walk away, Mandy says, "Stop locking me out of the apartment. I live there, too."

My temper flares as I spin around on my heel. "The hell you do! I pay the bills."

"We're family," she argues. "If it weren't for me, you wouldn't even be alive."

"Jesus," I huff, throwing my arms wide at my sides. "I don't owe you anything for giving birth to me, and being related by blood doesn't mean shit." Pointing a finger at her, my words are clipped as I say, "Stay away from my apartment, and the next time you steal my stuff, I'm calling the cops."

Mandy jumps to her feet and pokes her finger against my chest. "You wouldn't dare."

Leaning closer until I can smell the stale booze on her breath, I say, "I will. Get the fuck out of my life."

"That's enough," Sylvia's voice suddenly lashes over us. "Jaden, throw Mandy out," she orders the cook, who could easily double as a bouncer.

"I've got money," Mandy argues, and when she tries to take a seat at the booth again, Jaden grabs her by the arm and hauls her out of the diner.

Sylvia gives me a stern look. "Don't bring your personal shit into my diner."

Even though I feel it wasn't my fault, I nod and begin to wipe off the booth where Mandy's filthy ass sat.

I keep glancing through the window at where Mandy is leaning against the wall beneath an awning. She should take a long walk in the rain. At least, it would wash the dirt off her.

Chapter 6

Dario

Walking into the restaurant Skylar recently opened, I grin from ear to ear as I glance around the establishment. The bamboo against the walls and lanterns hanging from the ceiling give the place a peaceful atmosphere.

I'm taken to an open table, and after I sit down, I dig my cell phone from my pocket and send a text message to Renzo so he'll know I'm here.

A minute later my friend comes walking toward me and joins me at the table.

I take in the happiness shining from his eyes and say, "You look much better now that the shit with Montes has been dealt with."

"I feel better."

Montes' organization was responsible for the murder of someone close to Renzo, and it unleashed the darkest parts of my friend. I'm glad to see he was able to find closure so he can move on with his life.

I glance around the seating area again, then say, "The place looks good. Where's Skylar?"

He nods his head toward the back of the room. "She's in the kitchen."

I let out a sigh, which is followed by a chuckle. "I don't know what to do with all the free time I have now that you're not taking it all up with your shit."

"If you're bored, I can give you work," he jokes. "I have a shipment of machine guns that needs to be checked."

"Fuck no. I'm not that bored."

A waiter comes to the table, and Renzo places an order for two tumblers of bourbon. Glancing at me, he asks, "You hungry?"

"I can eat." The waiter offers me a menu which I decline. "I'll have Skylar's signature dish."

"I'll just have the bourbon," Renzo tells the waiter before he focuses his attention on me again. "How are things with the opera house and ballet company?"

"It's getting busy as we get closer to the winter show." I raise an eyebrow at my friend. "Are you going to come to opening night?"

I expect him to decline because none of the guys understands my obsession with the arts.

"Sure. Skylar and I will be there." I give Renzo a surprised look, which has him saying, "It's the least I can do to repay you for everything you've done for me the past few months." His eyes lock with mine. "If it weren't for you, I'm not sure I would've made it through the shitstorm."

His heartfelt words make me feel emotional, and I clear my throat as I shift in the chair.

To break the sappy moment between us, I mutter, "I knew you loved me."

Renzo makes a snorting sound just as the server brings our drinks.

We both take a couple of sips of the amber liquid before he asks, "You still watching that ballerina like some crazy-ass stalker?"

I give him a playful glare before admitting, "She isn't one of my ballerinas, and I haven't seen her in a couple of weeks. I've tried to find her, but the woman is like a ghost."

Renzo gives me an incredulous look. "You're not able to find her? Seriously?"

"I've been checking the CCTV cameras in the area, and a couple of the shots I've managed to find of her never show her face."

The corner of Renzo's mouth lifts slightly as he says, "The fact that you've tried to track her down tells me you have a serious hard-on for the woman."

I let out a burst of laughter before taking a sip of my drink. Swallowing the strong alcohol, I shrug. "It won't be the end of the world if I don't find her. I'm just intrigued to find out more about her."

Renzo's gaze narrows on me. "If you say so."

Skylar coming out of the kitchen with a tray of food draws our attention.

"Hi, Dario," she greets me with a smile.

A smile curves my lips as I climb to my feet, and after she places the tray on the table, I lean in to give her a quick hug.

"Hey. How are you doing, *bellissima*?" I ask, using the term of endearment to get a reaction from Renzo.

"Stop calling her that," he growls as he grips his woman's hand so he can tug her closer to him.

Laughing at my friend, I sit down again and grab my bowl of spicy Korean brisket.

"Damn, it smells mouthwatering," I compliment Skylar.

"Wait until you taste it," Renzo says with pride on his face.

"I need to get back to the kitchen," Skylar mentions. She presses a kiss to Renzo's mouth before leaving.

I dig into my food, and on my second bite, Renzo pulls a small box out of his pocket. Opening it, he asks, "What do you think of the ring?"

I almost choke on the food before I quickly swallow, and unable to resist, I exclaim, "Oh my God. I thought you'd never ask."

When I reach for the box, Renzo slaps my hand away and mutters, "It's for Skylar, dipshit."

Laughing, I take a closer look. "I think she'll love it. When are you proposing?"

"I'm not. I'm going to ask her to be my girlfriend. Plus, there's a tracker in the ring, so I can track her at all times."

"So romantic," I drawl. Pretending to be Renzo, I mock him, "Here's a tracker, *bellissima*. It's a token of my undying obsession with you."

He scowls at me as he tucks the small box back into his pocket. "I'm not going to say it like that. I've even ordered flowers."

"I'm just fucking with you," I say. "The ring is beautiful, and I think it's cute that you're asking her to be your girlfriend when you've already been dating for months."

"Cute, my ass," he grumbles. Glaring at me again, he adds, "Not everyone is as romantic as you."

I wag my eyebrows at him. "I know. That's what makes me such a catch."

"Yet, your ass is still single," he taunts me.

"By choice." To rile him up again, I add, "I let you have Skylar."

A dark frown settles on my friend's face. "The fuck you just say?"

When I start to laugh, Renzo reaches across the table in an attempt to slap me upside the head, but I jerk away just in time to avoid his hand.

He settles back in his chair and mutters, "You can be glad you're one of my favorite people, or you'd be dead right now."

His phone begins to ring, and as he pulls the device out of his pocket, he gets up and says, "Enjoy the rest of your meal."

I nod, and when he walks toward the back, where the offices are so he can take the call, I continue eating.

I'm surprised Renzo's not asking Skylar to marry him, but then again, they've only known each other a few months and had one hell of a rocky start.

I'm more like Angelo in that regard. When I find the woman I want to spend my life with, I'll tie her to me as quickly as humanly possible.

My elusive dancer pops into my mind's eye, and tapping my fingers on the table's surface, I wonder if I'll get to see her again or whether I scared her off for good with the kiss.

Chapter 7

Eden

Walking up the street toward the ballet company, I pull my coat tighter around my body in an attempt to ward off the cold front that hit New York early this morning.

It's colder than usual for this time of year, which means we're going to shit ice cubes this winter.

Suddenly, an expensive sports car with dark-tinted windows comes to a screeching stop a couple of feet ahead of me, and when the driver's door opens, and a man steps out, I freeze in my tracks.

Shit. Dario.

I spin around and walk as fast as I can away from him, but I only manage a few steps before he darts in front of me. He grips hold of my arm, his hold a little too tight for my liking.

"Finally," he breathes. "I thought I wouldn't see you again."

Well, I did try my best to avoid you.

I glance down at his fingers around my arm, then say, "Can you let go of me?"

"No."

His reply shocks me and causes a frown to form on my forehead.

Dario looks around us, and the next second, he drags me across the street toward a Starbucks.

"Hey," I snap.

"Just have coffee with me, then I'll let you go."

I glance over my shoulder to where his car is parked in a no-parking zone.

"They're going to tow your car away," I mention in the hopes that I can get out having coffee with him because I need to get my ass to work.

"I don't care," he mutters.

Once inside the warm coffee shop, I'm pulled to a table and practically shoved down in a chair.

I glare at Dario as he takes a seat across from me. "If you manhandle me again, I'm going to knee you in your balls."

Much to my surprise, he lets out an amused chuckle. His eyes shine with a mischievous look, which makes me think he's not taking me seriously.

"You won't be the first guy I bring to his knees," I mutter while crossing my arms over my chest.

"*Tesoro*, the day I'm on my knees in front of you, it will be because I'm eating your pussy and not because you managed to knee me."

Holy shit.

My mouth drops open, and I can only gape at the man and his filthy mouth.

A triumphant smile curves his lips. "Good. Now that I have your attention, I have a few questions I need answered."

My eyebrows lift, and I finally find my tongue again. "What makes you think I'm going to answer questions?"

His gaze narrows enough for me to know he means every word when he says, "I will tie you to that chair if I have to, but you're not leaving here until I have my answers."

"Geez, demanding much?" My body relaxes in the chair, and I glance at the menu on the wall. "I want a hot chocolate." My eyes latch onto the display counter that's loaded with all kinds of delicious desserts. "And I want a chocolate chip cookie and a slice of cheesecake. The dessert is to go for later."

I want to give the cake to Tyrone to say thank you for always being there for me, and I might as well make Dario pay for it.

"If you make a run for it, I swear I will tackle you off your feet," he warns me.

I wave a hand at the counter. "Just go get my hot chocolate."

There's a weary look on his face as he gets up, and as soon as he walks to the counter, I pull my cell phone out and send a quick text to Quincy, who's the security guard at the company.

I'll be thirty minutes late. A huge chocolate chip cookie from Starbucks is yours if you cover for me.

I glance at where Dario's placing the order before my attention is pulled back to my phone as a message comes through.

Quincy: I got you covered.

I put my phone away and look at Dario again. It's only now that I take a moment to drink in the sight of the man, and damn, he looks better than I remember.

Even though I've been avoiding him, I haven't stopped thinking about him.

Or the kiss we shared.

I have to admit a part of me feels super flattered that he's giving me attention.

When he returns to the table with two drinks and my desserts in a paper bag, I pick up the glass and take a sip of the sweet and warm beverage.

God, just what I needed.

Dario adds sugar into his black expresso as he says, "First question. What's your name?"

I play with the idea of giving him a fake name, but in the end, I mutter, "Eden."

A sexy-as-hell smile curves his lips up. "I've never met anyone with that name before. It suits you."

"It better suit me. I'm stuck with it for life." I start to feel bad for being so bitchy but worrying about getting to work and not blowing my cover is pushing my stress level to its limit.

Dario relaxes in his chair, and with his eyes locked on my face, he murmurs in a deep and rough voice, "Eden."

My abdomen clenches so hard I shift in my seat and look everywhere but at him.

"Were you heading to the studio when I stopped you?" he asks.

Shit.

I quickly shake my head. "No, I don't go there anymore."

"Why?"

Because I'd like to keep my job and not get fired.

"Ah...I don't have time." I hate lying, but paying the bills is more important than my moral ethics.

"Why are you avoiding looking at me?" he asks.

My eyes snap to his way too handsome face. "I'm not."

He tilts his head as he fires another question in my direction. "Why did you run after the kiss?"

Ooooh damn.

I spit out the first thing that comes to mind. "It was either run or fuck you right there on the floor."

"I would've been fine with the latter." Dario's eyes narrow on my face as if he's trying to see into my soul. "It's clear the attraction is mutual, yet you avoid me. Why?"

Because you own the company I work for.

The pressure I'm feeling makes laughter burst over my lips while I try to think of an answer to give him.

"What's so funny?" Dario asks.

I try to rein in the laughter while shaking my head. "It's a weird thing I do when I'm in trouble or feel awkward."

"You're not in trouble, and you don't seem like someone who gets awkward," he states. "Is there another reason?"

I take a sip of my hot chocolate, then mutter, "Can we change the subject?"

"You still owe me an answer," he reminds me.

Now that I've had time to think, I realize I don't have to lie as I tell him the truth. "I'm avoiding you because I'm not looking for a fling."

"Who said anything about a fling?" Dario asks.

Annoyed by all the questions and needing to get my ass to work, I grab the paper bag, but before I can get up, Dario grabs hold of my wrist.

"I need to go," I say, my tone tense from this little encounter.

"I'll let you go if you give me your phone number," he tries to make a deal.

I think about it for a moment, then let out a sigh. "Fine."

I wait for him to pull his cell phone from his pocket before I rattle my number off to him.

Giving his hand around my wrist a pointed look, I mutter, "A deal's a deal."

When he lets go, I meet his eyes for a moment, which is a mistake because I instantly feel the intense pull between us.

"I'll call you soon," he says as he picks up his cup of coffee.

I stare at Dario for a few seconds longer before I turn around and rush out of the Starbucks.

Just as I step out onto the sidewalk, my phone starts to ring. I pull the device out of my pocket, and thinking it's Quincy calling to tell me to get my ass to work, I don't look at the screen and answer, "Hey."

"Just making sure you gave me the right number before you disappear from my sight," Dario's voice rumbles in my ear.

Glancing over my shoulder, I see him watching me through the window.

"Okay. Bye." I end the call, and pushing the device back into my pocket, I walk as fast as I can toward the ballet company.

Knowing Dario is probably heading in the same direction, I walk around the back, where I give the security camera a pleading look.

I hope Quincy sees me on the security feed.

And here, I've done my best to make sure my face is always hidden from the cameras around the building.

All for nothing.

When five minutes pass, I worry I'll have no choice but to use the main entrance. Just as I start to walk away, the door clicks open, and Quincy asks, "Why are you using this door?"

"I'm avoiding someone." I enter the building and dig the chocolate cookie from the paper bag. "Here you go."

"Just in time for my coffee break."

I hurry to the staff locker room and quickly put on my apron and cap. Retrieving my cleaning cart, I check that I have all the supplies I'll need, and only when I push the cart toward the auditorium do I manage to let out a relieved breath.

My mind starts racing with thoughts of my interaction with Dario.

God, I was so rude to the man.

Feeling bad, I pull my cell phone out and type a quick message to him.

Eden: Sorry for being so rude. You just caught me at a bad time.

I watch as he instantly reads the message, then it shows he's typing.

Dario: At least I caught you.

A smile tugs at my lips.

Dario: Have dinner with me on Friday.

My smile fades, and I stare at the message for a while before I type my reply.

Eden: I'm busy Friday night, but I can squeeze you in on Sunday.

Dario: Sunday works for me. Send me your address so I can pick you up.

My eyebrows fly up, and I shake my head as my fingers fly over my phone's keyboard.

Eden: I'm not telling a perfect stranger where I live. I'll meet you somewhere.

Dario: Six pm at Yukhaejang.

I've never heard of the place.

I quickly Google the name and see it's a restaurant. Going back to my messenger app, I send Dario another text.

Eden: I'll be there.

Dario: Just so there's no misunderstanding, it's a date.

I stare at the words, torn between feeling excited and worried.

A date with Dario La Rosa.

What am I doing?

Chapter 8

Dario

When I leave Starbucks, I glance up the street and see Eden walking right past the ballet company.

I stare at her for a moment before a whining sound draws my attention to my right. Seeing a dog with the leash tied to a fire hydrant, I walk closer.

I crouch in front of the dog and carefully pet her head. "I'm just going to assume you're a girl," I whisper as my palm brushes over her soft hair. "What are you doing out here in the cold?"

She jumps up against me with her two front paws, drawing a chuckle from me.

I glance around as I rise to my feet, but when I take a step in the direction of my car, something twists in my gut, and I look at the dog again.

She's staring at me with the biggest brown eyes I've ever seen, making my heart melt on the spot.

"Keep looking at me like that, and I'm going to kidnap you," I warn the dog as if she can understand me.

I look into the Starbucks through the window and wonder which of the patrons the dog belongs to.

Deciding to pet her until the owner shows up, I crouch down again and let the dog sniff my hand before I scratch a spot behind her ear.

"I should get a dog," I tell her. I look at her fluffy, long ears and white and brown coat. "What breed are you?"

I begin to feel uncomfortable crouching for so long and rise to my full height again.

When fifteen minutes have passed with no sign of the owner, I begin to feel very annoyed.

Who leaves their dog out in the cold for so long?

And with no water.

A frown settles on my forehead as I glance down at the dog. "I'm seriously considering kidnapping you."

Compared to shit the other heads of the Cosa Nostra have done, kidnapping a dog ranks low on shitty things to do.

I glance around the area and into the Starbucks, and when it doesn't look like anyone is in a hurry to get back to the furry animal, I untie her leash and pick her up.

"That's it. You belong to me now," I mutter as I walk to where my car is parked.

The fact that no one tries to stop me pisses me off even more.

I press the fob, and when the doors unlock, I open the driver's side and get into the R8. I place the dog on the passenger seat before I shut the door and start the engine.

I keep glancing at my kidnap victim, but she seems happy where she's looking out the window with her tail wagging.

Angelo forced Vittoria to marry him, and Renzo kidnapped Skylar.

Me? I steal a dog.

I shake my head at myself as a chuckle escapes me.

My thoughts turn to Eden, which makes my smile grow wider.

I have a date with my elusive dancer.

Fuck, I thought I was hallucinating the woman when I saw her walking on the side of the road. I slammed on the brakes so fast I almost gave myself whiplash.

I don't stop at the ballet company like I was planning on doing and drive in the direction of my apartment.

"I should probably stop somewhere and get you food before we go home," I mutter.

Pulling my phone out of my pocket, I check for nearby pet stores.

"Found one on Maddison Ave," I say as I glance at the dog, who's staring at me with her mouth wide open while she pants.

It looks like she's smiling at me, and once again, my heart melts into a puddle.

When I stop at the store, I scoop the dog into my arms, and after climbing out of the car, I quickly check whether my new pet is male or female.

"I was right." I grin at her. "You're a girl."

She licks my jaw, and I'm overcome with cuteness aggression, almost squashing the furball too hard to my chest.

Walking into the store, I head to the counter and smile at the attendant. "I just got a dog and need the best of everything."

The attendant gets to work, and after ten minutes, I worry how I'll get everything home. The R8 doesn't have a big trunk, and it's only a two-seater.

I dig my cell phone out and dial Renzo's number.

"Hey," he answers the call.

"I need you to come to a pet store with an SUV," I tell him.

"A pet store? Why?"

"I kidnapped a dog and need help getting all her things to my apartment."

"You kidnapped a dog," he deadpans. "Are you joking or serious?"

"I'm serious."

"Oh...okay."

The call ends, and I quickly send the address before I grin at my fur ball.

What am I going to call her?

I stare into her eyes. "How about I call you *Bellissima*?"

She rubs her head against my shoulder while her body wiggles in my hold.

"You like that, right?" Again, she wiggles, and I squish her to my chest. "Fuck, I'm going to crush you if you keep being so cute."

"Do you want clothes for your dog?" the store attendant asks.

"Yes." I follow her to where there are all kinds of clothes and adorable stuff. "I want pink bows to put in her hair."

While the attendant grabs a variety of bows, I walk back to the counter and grab one of the new bowls. "Where can I get some water?"

"I'll fill the bowl," she says.

While she's getting water, I open a box of bone-shaped biscuits and feed one to *Bellissima*.

I see Renzo double park beside my R8, and when he comes into the store, he actually looks shocked.

"I didn't think you were serious," he mutters as he stares at my dog.

The attendant brings the bowl, and I set *Bellissima* down on the floor so she can drink some water.

Keeping hold of the leash, I pull out my wallet and hand my black credit card to the attendant.

Renzo signals for Vincenzo to come help while Fabrizio remains in the SUV. He never goes anywhere without the two men.

The other four heads of the Cosa Nostra have all said I need to get guards, but I never got around to it.

Honestly, I'm not the biggest threat out of the five of us, and someone has to be fucking stupid to come after me knowing the Cosa Nostra will retaliate.

When the payment goes through, the attendant hands me my card. I crouch to pick up *Bellissima* and the bowl.

Walking out of the store, I empty the remaining water on the sidewalk and head to my car.

"I'm going to charge you a delivery fee," Renzo calls out as he heads back to the SUV.

"You're going to charge me for helping bring your goddaughter's stuff to the apartment?"

"Now I'm the godfather of a dog? Did you drink too much today?"

I climb into the R8 and place *Bellissima* on the passenger seat. Starting the engine, I have to wait for the SUV to move before I can pull away from the curb.

As soon as there's a gap in traffic, I floor the gas, and the R8 shoots around the SUV, leaving them behind.

Bellissima lets out a bark as she slides across the seat, and I instantly decelerate.

"Sorry, Daddy didn't mean to make you lose your balance," I apologize to her.

Fifteen minutes later, I bring the car to a stop in my parking bay, and as I pick up *Bellissima* and climb out of the vehicle, Renzo's SUV comes to a standstill next to me.

I give Fabrizio a chin lift and grab the bag with *Bellissima's* clothes. The men bring the other bags and dog bed, and we all pile into the elevator.

When we step into my apartment, I say, "Just put everything in the living room."

I set *Bellissima* down on a couch and say, "This is your new home."

Esmerelda, my housekeeper, comes out of the kitchen, and when she sees the dog on the leather couch, a frown forms on her forehead.

"Animals don't belong on couches," she complains. "She'll scratch the leather."

"Then I'll buy a new couch."

I grin at my fur ball, then leaning over her, I pet the living shit out of her. She turns onto her back, and I can see how much she loves belly scratches.

"*Bellissima* lives here now," I inform Esmerelda. Rising to my full height, I glance at her. "I got dry dog food, but I want you to make fresh food for her as well."

I can see she's not happy about cooking for a dog, but she won't dare argue with me on the matter.

Renzo glances from me to *Bellissima*. "Why did you kidnap the dog?"

"Someone left her tied to a fire hydrant out in the cold."

"Oh no," Esmerelda gasps. "People can be so cruel. I'll make some chicken for her."

My housekeeper disappears back into the kitchen, and I know it's only a matter of time before she falls in love with *Bellissima*.

"So just like that, I have a goddaughter?" he asks.

"Yep."

"What are you going to name her?"

I know the term of endearment annoys the fuck out of him, so my grin is extra wide when I reply, "*Bellissima*."

He gives me a disgruntled look. "You like that word way too much." He steps closer to my dog and rubs behind her left ear. "And it's a long name for such a small dog. She looks more like a Bella."

Liking the sound of the name, I nod. "I like that. Bella."

Renzo picks up my dog, and it has me saying, "Don't even think about it. She's mine."

"I'm just holding her," he mutters. "Damn, if you're so possessive over a dog you just got, I don't want to see you when you fall for a woman."

Chapter 9

Eden

While I'm walking around the diner, refilling coffee wherever I see an empty cup, I keep thinking it's insane that I agreed to a date with Dario.

Yep. Totally insane.

So much could go wrong.

He could find out I'm a janitor at his company and fire my ass.

He could find out I'm poorer than a church mouse, and that won't look good for his image.

He could find out I have a drug addict leech for a mother. That will definitely have him dumping my ass if we ever make it past the first date.

I've thought about canceling but can never bring myself to do it.

When I place the coffee pot back on the counter, my phone begins to ring in my pocket. I dig it out, and seeing Dario's name, surprise rushes through me.

Walking to Sherrie, I say, "I'm just taking a quick break. Five minutes."

"Okay."

I accept the call as I rush through the kitchen and out the back into an alley. "Hi."

"You answered," Dario says, sounding surprised.

"Ahh...wasn't I supposed to?"

He lets out a chuckle that vibrates through my ear, sending a wave of tingles over my body.

"How are you?" he asks.

"Good." I glance up and down the alley before toeing the little step by the backdoor with the tip of my sneaker. "And you?"

"I'm doing great."

I hear him breathing, and it makes a weird fluttering erupt in my stomach.

This is crazy. How can a man affect me just by breathing?

"Where are you?" Dario asks.

"At work."

"Where's work?"

I push my free hand into the back pocket of my jeans. "Not telling you."

"Okay. What do you do for a living?"

I let out a chuckle. "Not telling you."

This time, his voice is deep and dripping with sex when he asks, "What are you willing to tell me?"

My mind races as I search for something to share, and my shoulders slump a little as I say, "I don't come from a rich family."

"Okay?"

He sounds puzzled, and it has me explaining, "I heard you have money, and people with money usually move in certain circles. I just want you to know I don't fit in with that crowd."

"I don't fit in with that crowd either," he says, which draws an incredulous-sounding chuckle from me. "You don't believe me," he states the obvious.

"It doesn't matter what I believe."

"Eden!" I hear Sylvia call from inside.

"I have to go."

Not waiting for Dario to respond, I end the call and rush back into the kitchen.

When Sylvia sees me, she gives me a look filled with warning. "Get your ass back out there. Sherrie and Destiny can't handle your section as well as their own."

"Sorry," I mutter as I rush past her, and when I see how busy it's gotten, I feel bad for taking the call.

We stay busy for the next two hours, and by the time I take off my apron, I'm dead on my feet.

Ugh, all I want to do is go to bed, but I have to rush over to Midtown if I don't want to be late for my night shift at the ballet company.

I grab the meatloaf and vegetables I asked Jaden to prepare when I started my shift, and walking to the door, I say, "See you tomorrow."

"Don't come in for the morning shift," Sylvia says as I pass by the counter where she's cashing up.

I stop dead in my tracks. "Why?"

"Because I have to give some of the other girls extra shifts. Everyone needs money around the holidays."

We're all in the same boat, struggling to survive another day.

Nodding, I leave the diner while my mind does calculation after calculation.

Shit, I need the extra money, or it's going to be one hell of a cold and long winter with no heat.

Taking the subway to Midtown, I keep worrying about finances, which is nothing new. I'll just have to find a third job somewhere.

When I get off the subway, I don't pay attention to my surroundings as I walk to work.

Suddenly, someone grabs my bag, and before I even register the sting across my shoulder, a man sets off with it.

"Hey!" I yell as I run after the asshole. "Give back my bag!"

When I realize he's faster than me, I stop, yank off my sneaker and throw it at him. The shoe whacks the man against his back, but it doesn't stop him from disappearing around a corner.

"Fucking asshole!" I shout at the top of my lungs. "I hope you die, you shit-eating pig."

I'm so angry my body is a trembling mess as I walk to where my sneaker is lying on the sidewalk.

After I pick it up and slip it back onto my foot, I realize people are staring at me, and it has me snapping, "What the hell are you all looking at? The show's over."

Pulling my cell phone out of my pocket, I look up the number for my bank and call them so they can put a hold on my account in case the asshole tries to use my card to steal the meager funds I have.

I walk to work, thinking about everything I have to replace, which upsets me even more.

Today sucks so bad!

When I get close to the ballet company, I glance around to make sure I don't see Dario's car, and not seeing it parked anywhere, I walk into the building.

"Hi, Quincy," I say as I stop by his desk. "Some asshole just stole my bag."

"That sucks," he mutters. "Stafford is on a warpath, so you better get to work."

"Thanks for the heads up," I mumble before heading to the back, where the staff's lockers are.

As I pull on my apron, my phone starts to ring, and I quickly dig it out of my pocket.

Seeing Tyrone's name, I answer, "Hey, what's up?"

"Two men were sniffing around your apartment and asking about Mandy."

Sinking down in a crouching position, I rub my palm over my forehead. "The bitch. I'm going to kill her when I see her again."

"Not if they get to her first. These men meant business, baby girl. Be careful when you come and go."

"I will."

We end the call, and I sit flat on my ass on the cold tiles as a hopeless feeling fills my chest. There's a lot I can endure, but today is starting to get the better of me.

Just as my luck would have it, the door opens, and Mrs. Stafford catches me sitting on the floor.

I quickly climb to my feet, but it's too late.

She levels me with an angry look. "I don't pay you to sit around doing nothing."

"Yes, ma'am."

"Bring a mop. One of the girls vomited."

Jesus, why do you hate me so much?

Chapter 10

Dario

With the winter show fast approaching, things are tense at the ballet company. We already lost two ballerinas because they couldn't handle the pressure.

And Mrs. Stafford has turned into a screeching banshee. Christ, the woman should've become a sergeant in the army. She sure as fuck has the lungs to shout out orders all day long.

Sitting in the auditorium during a rehearsal, the usual peace I get to experience is nowhere to be found.

"No! No! No!" Mrs. Stafford shouts while stomping her foot. "What have you all been learning in class? I have more grace in my pinky than you lot are displaying. Start over."

Having had enough, I stand up and walk to the front row, where Mrs. Stafford is taking a seat.

When she looks up at me, I say, "I think you should take a break. Go home."

"What?" she gasps as she climbs back to her feet. "The show is in three weeks!"

I give her a look of warning, then murmur, "Never raise your voice at me."

She quickly collects herself and forces a quivering smile to her face. "I apologize, Mr. La Rosa."

When she walks away, I turn to the stage and call out, "Everyone take a fifteen-minute break."

Needing to get everyone under control so the show won't be an epic failure, I walk out of the auditorium and go after Mrs. Stafford.

When I come around a corner it's to see her laying into one of the janitors.

"You can't mop the floor when we're all still here. What if one of the ballerinas slips and breaks a leg?"

I can't hear what the janitor is mumbling, and when I get to them, I glance at the poor woman, but I can't see her face because the cap she's wearing is in the way.

Locking eyes with Mrs. Stafford, I say, "Your office. Now."

When I walk away, I hear something fall from the cleaning cart.

"You almost spilled bleach on my shoes!"

Losing my shit, my voice is harsh as I snap, "Mrs. Stafford, stop screeching at everyone and go to the office."

Not waiting, I stalk to the office and shove the door open. Pacing the floor, I take a deep breath so I'll calm down because I can't afford to fire Mrs. Stafford this close to the show.

She comes into the office and shuts the door so we'll have privacy.

I take another deep breath before saying, "I won't tolerate you screaming at my ballerinas and staff. Everyone is stressed out, and you're making it worse."

"I apologize, Mr. La Rosa," she murmurs. "The pressure got to me."

"Take tomorrow off and get some rest. I'll handle the rehearsals until you return." When it looks like she's going to argue, I shake my head. "It's an order."

She walks to her desk to retrieve her handbag, and before she leaves the office, she asks, "I'll take the night to compose myself, but please let me return tomorrow. I've worked the whole year for this show."

"Fine, but if I hear you screaming at one more person, it will cost you your job," I warn her.

I can see my threat hit her hard, and she walks out of the office with a trembling chin.

As silence falls around me, I feel fucking agitated.

I don't lose my shit a lot, but if there's one thing that pisses me off, it's people mistreating others.

I need to calm down.

I wouldn't mind watching Eden dance instead of returning to the rehearsal.

When an idea pops into my head, I pull my phone out of my pocket and dial Eden's number. I'm hoping I can talk her into dancing for me tonight. I swear if she says yes, I'm sending everyone home.

"Hi?" she answers, sounding a little apprehensive.

"Please come to the ballet company and dance for me."

"What?"

"Come dance for me, Eden."

"Ahh…I'm kinda busy right now."

"I'll wait."

She's quiet for so long that I check the phone's screen to make sure she didn't hang up on me.

"Aren't you busy preparing for some kind of show?"

"Yes, but I can send everyone home."

She's quiet again, and it has me saying, "I'll pay you. Name your price."

"To dance? You've got some of the best ballerinas at your company. Why not ask one of them?"

"None of them are you."

I hear her breathing then she says, "Fine. I'll be there in an hour."

I suck in a relieved breath when she agrees, and a smile spreads over my face.

Eden hangs up, and I tuck the device into my pocket as I leave the office.

I head back to the auditorium so I can tell everyone to go home. I want this place emptied out as quickly as possible.

Sitting in the studio, I keep checking the time, which is fucking crawling by at a snail's pace.

The moment Eden walks into the room, wearing her tight shorts and cropped shirt, relief floods my body again.

I switch off my phone and put it away while my eyes follow her every movement as she walks to the desk, where she sets her phone down after connecting it to the speakers.

She stands still for a moment, and when the music starts to play, she turns around and looks at me.

Just from the opening notes I recognize *Never Enough* by *Lauren Allred*. It's one of my favorites, and I've lost count of how many times I've watched *The Greatest Showman.*

Eden walks toward me, and when she's close enough, she lifts her hand and rests her palm against my jaw. It looks like turbulent storms are brewing in her eyes.

Something upset her today.

The thought makes a protective feeling for her explode in my chest.

Our gazes remain locked for an intense moment before she suddenly spins away from me. Her body twirls and twirls, and it makes the music a million times more intense.

My heart instantly thunders in my chest, and the stress of the upcoming show fades away like mist before the sun until there's only Eden.

She dances with so much aggression and passion it captures me in a trance.

In the middle of the room, she jumps into the air before falling like a dead weight to the floor as if something yanked her down. I dart up from my chair, thinking she got hurt, but she claws at the floor as if it's keeping her imprisoned before she leaps to her feet in a single fluid motion I've never seen before.

With parted lips, I watch Eden express so much emotion I'm stunned speechless.

Pompeii begins to play, and she keeps dancing.

I sit down again, my eyes not leaving her for a single second as one song flows into the next.

I've seen awe-inspiring shows and the best of the best on a stage, but none of them compare to her.

I have no idea how much time has passed when she stops in the middle of the floor, completely out of breath.

Lifting her head, her eyes lock with mine.

The ever-present tension between us sparks to life until I feel it vibrating in the air.

Even though I hardly know anything about her, I want this woman more than my next breath.

Eden walks toward me, and I'm just about to stand up, but she places her hand on my shoulder, and I remain seated.

Her eyes lower to my mouth, and the intensity between us spikes dangerously high.

As I grip hold of her hips, she straddles me and crushes her mouth to mine.

Christ.

The intensity of emotions she evokes in me almost becomes unbearable.

My hands roam up her sweaty body as I take control of the kiss. My tongue massages hers to the beat of the music, and when she reaches for the zipper of my pants, I push her up and drag her shorts and panties down her legs.

I hardly get to look at her pussy before she's straddling me again and rushing to free my cock.

Our mouths come together in a crash, and I have zero control of my body when I feel the heat of her pussy press against the head of my cock. I grip her hips tightly and thrust hard into her wet entrance.

"Oh God," she sobs against my mouth when I'm only halfway inside her.

Eden's hips jerk and gyrate while desperate need rolls off her in waves, making me realize she needs this moment as much as I do.

I pull out a little before thrusting harder inside her until I'm buried as deep as her body will take me.

At some point, we stop kissing, our breaths warming the inch of space between us.

Her beautiful gray eyes focus on mine then she begins to move on my lap to the beat of *You Say* by *Lauren Allred*. It's not a well-known song, and the fact that it's on Eden's playlist makes me even more curious about her.

I'm fucking entranced by the woman as she fucks me, and as her hips gyrate faster and faster, the intimacy between us builds to a crescendo.

When her features tighten and her fingers curl into my shoulders, the strangest emotion I've ever felt creeps into my heart.

I watch as Eden comes, completely hypnotized by the soft whimper falling over her lips.

Her body strains against mine as I speed up the pace to chase my own release.

Pleasure shoots through my abdomen, and a groan is ripped from my chest as I orgasm deep inside her.

We keep staring at each other as ecstacy fills the air around us, but just as I start to come down from my release, Eden pulls free from me.

She grabs her panties and shorts, and as she drags them up her legs, I say, "Don't run."

"I have to go."

I tuck my cock back into my pants, and shooting to my feet, I grab hold of her arm before she can hightail it out of the studio.

Eden's eyes snap to my face. "I'm not running away. I really have to go."

"Where do you keep running off to?"

She lets out a sigh, then admits, "Work."

A frown forms on my forehead as I ask, "What kind of work?"

In my world, nothing good happens at night.

Not answering me, she pulls her arm free from my hold and walks to the other side of the room to get her phone. The music stops, and when she heads to the door, she asks, "Are we still on for Sunday?"

I nod as I close the distance between us. "Definitely."

Eden doesn't dart away, but instead, a smile curves her lips. "Thanks for asking me to dance tonight. I needed it."

A grin spreads over my face as I lean down to press a kiss to her mouth before murmuring near her ear, "The pleasure was all mine."

When I pull back, she walks out of the studio.

I take a moment to tuck my shirt back into my pants before pulling up my zipper. Digging my phone out of my pocket, I turn the device on as I leave the room.

Seeing I have a missed call from Damiano, I quickly dial his number.

When he answers, he asks, "What took you so long to call me back?"

"I was having sex," I reply with a massive smile on my face.

The man doesn't even respond to what I just told him and orders, "There's a meeting at my club at nine tomorrow morning."

"I'll be there."

The second I end the call, my thoughts are inundated with Eden and what happened between us tonight.

My first instinct is to go home so I can search for every little piece of information I can find out about her, but something keeps me from doing that.

I don't want to invade her privacy.

For the first time, I actually want to take the time to get to know a woman. I want her to tell and show me who she is.

Exiting the building, I head to where my car is parked, and as I open the door, something I haven't considered pops into my mind.

If things get serious between Eden and me, how the hell am I going to tell her I'm a part of the Cosa Nostra?

Chapter 11

Eden

The floor polisher's handle vibrates in my grip while I stare at nothing in particular.

The past twenty-four hours have left me feeling rattled. First, I lost the morning shift at the diner, then my bag was stolen. I had to clean up puke and got scolded, time and time again, by Mrs. Stafford.

I agreed to dance for Dario because I needed to ease the stress bearing down on my shoulders, but I didn't plan to have sex with him. That just kind of happened.

I was so wrapped up in the moment that I didn't stop to think about what I was doing.

I wouldn't classify it as a one-night stand, and even if it was, it wouldn't be my first.

But I was reckless. We didn't use protection, and although I'm on birth control, I should be more careful of catching an STD.

I'm sure Dario's clean, and out of everything I have to worry about, an STD isn't at the top of my list. To ease some of my stress, I pull my phone out and send him a message.

Eden: Are you clean, or should I get checked out?

Not even a minute later, my phone vibrates.

Dario: I'm clean. Are you on birth control?

Eden: Yes.

Dario: I'll make sure to carry condoms for the next time.

A chuckle escapes me.

Eden: You assume there will be a next time.

Dario: You blew my mind. There will definitely be a second...third...fourth...fifth...etc.

Eden: It all depends on how the date goes.

Dario: Then I'll just have to impress you.

After messaging Dario, I feel a little better, and while I do my work, I keep replaying the night over and over in my mind.

The sex was hot and emotional, which is something I haven't experienced before. I'm used to quick fucks with men who don't care whether I orgasm.

Jesus, Dario didn't even have to try. Just having him inside me was enough to make me come.

I can still feel his hands roaming my body. I can still taste him. I can still smell his scent on me.

And now I'm getting hot and bothered again.

With a smile playing around my mouth, I keep thinking about Dario until I'm done with my work. After putting away the cleaning cart and equipment, I go to the locker room, where I take off the apron and cap.

I check my locker for my bag only to remember it was stolen.

Shit.

My apartment's keys were in the bag.

I slam the locker shut, and as I walk to the exit, I realize I don't have money for the subway.

Feeling miserable, I stop by Quincy's desk and say, "I hate asking, but can I borrow ten dollars? I'll pay you back tonight."

"Sure." He digs the bill out of his wallet, and I take it with a grateful smile.

"Be careful on your way home." He says the same thing every morning because the streets aren't the safest at two am.

"I will," I reply, shooting him a smile. "Thanks for the money." I walk to the side door and wait for Quincy to buzz me out.

A blast of chilly air slaps me right in the face, and I huddle into my coat as I walk in the direction of the subway.

Now that I've left work, the bubble I was caught in pops, and I realize how stupid I was to have sex with Dario. I'm not so sure going on a date with him will be a good idea.

What if he wants more, and things get serious between us? What if he finds out I'm nothing but a poor girl from the wrong side of the city?

I seriously doubt he's going to want to keep seeing me. Things like that only happen in the movies.

But maybe…?

I shake my head, and glancing up and down the street, I quickly cross to the other side before I take the steps down to the subway.

Even though it's two-thirty in the morning, there are still people around. Everyone looks tired, and it makes the atmosphere somber.

It takes another forty-five minutes before I reach my apartment, and knowing the window by the fire escape is nailed shut, I have no choice but to wake up Tyrone.

I head into the building, and as I take the stairs up, I dial Tyrone's number.

His voice is groggy with sleep as he answers, "What happened? Are you okay?"

"I'm fine. My bag was stolen, and I can't get into my apartment. Can I crash on your couch?"

"Of course."

Just as I reach the third floor, Tyrone's front door opens, and I walk inside. I wait for him to lock behind us before I move closer and plant my head against his chest while wrapping my arms around him.

"I need a hug," I mutter as tears threaten to overwhelm me.

I'm so tired.

Tyrone rubs a comforting hand up and down my back for a while before he says, "Get some sleep, baby girl. When the hardware store opens, I'll get a new lock for your door and change it."

Pulling away, I force a smile to my face. "Thanks, Tyrone. I don't know what I'd do without you."

A fatherly smile curves his lips up. "Luckily for you, you'll never have to find out. I plan on sticking around for a long time."

"You better."

I walk to the couch and kick off my sneakers before lying down. A few seconds later, Tyrone places two blankets over me.

He presses a kiss to the side of my head, then murmurs, "Get some sleep."

When he walks back to his bedroom, I say, "Tyrone."

"Yeah?"

"I love you."

"Love you too, baby girl."

When I see *Yukhaejang*, the restaurant where I'm meeting Dario, I stop walking.

I glance up and down the street for the R8 I've seen him drive, but the car isn't parked anywhere.

Pulling my phone out, I check the time. It's almost six, but there's no way I'm going into the restaurant only to be stood up.

I wait a few minutes, and when six comes and goes and there's no sign of Dario's car, a weird feeling sinks into my stomach.

I walk closer to the restaurant, and just to be sure he's not here, I glance through the window.

When I don't see Dario, I realize how much I was looking forward to the date.

Ugh. I even put on a skirt and stockings for the man. The heels on my feet are uncomfortable, and it makes me feel angry that I went through all this trouble to look pretty for the date.

Turning around, I walk back in the direction of the subway while sending him a text.

Eden: You could've saved me the trouble and just canceled instead of standing me up.

I'm surprised when I see him read the message immediately, and I stop walking.

Not even a second later, my phone starts ringing.

"Hi," I mutter.

"Care to explain the message you sent?"

Hearing his deep voice sends tingles rushing over my body.

"It's already twenty past six, and you're not here."

"I am. Where are you?"

Shocked, I swing around and start walking back to the restaurant while saying, "I didn't see your car, and you weren't sitting at any of the tables."

"Where are you?" he asks again.

"A block away from the restaurant."

Dario hangs up on me, and tucking the device back into my pocket, I can't keep from smiling because he didn't stood me up.

A couple of seconds later, Dario comes out of the restaurant and glances up and down the street. When his eyes land on me, he doesn't wait but walks toward me.

Every step he takes is filled with determination, and it makes a kaleidoscope of butterflies erupt in my stomach.

Unlike the suit he usually wears, he's dressed in a pair of faded black jeans and a dark gray sweater that looks expensive but cozy.

As soon as he's in hearing distance, I say, "Sorry, I thought you ditched me."

Without a word, his arm slips around my lower back. I'm tugged flush with his chest, and his mouth crushes against mine.

All I can do is grab hold of his biceps while he kisses the ever-loving shit out of me.

It's so intense I forget about the people around us and don't hear the sounds of the city.

When he breaks the kiss, he pulls back until our eyes lock. He brings a hand to my face, and his thumb brushes over my bottom lip.

It takes me a moment to catch my bearings, then I ask, "What was that for?"

"Just want to make sure there's no misunderstanding between us. I want to get to know you better, and one fuck isn't enough for me."

I love the intensity coming off him, and I can't stop a smile from forming around my lips. "Okay."

Dario takes hold of my hand and leads me to the restaurant. When we walk inside, I glance around the place, thinking it looks expensive.

Then again, everything's expensive to me.

When he takes me to a private room, I understand why I didn't see him sitting at any of the tables. It almost feels like I've stepped into a bamboo forest with soft, warm lights coming from lanterns.

"It's pretty."

"I'm glad you like it," Dario murmurs as he pulls a chair out for me.

A server comes in and smiles at me. "Can I take your coat, ma'am?"

Wow. Fancy.

I shrug out of my coat and hand it to him.

When I sit down, Dario's eyes drift over me with a look that tells me he appreciates what he's seeing.

"You look beautiful."

I glance at my skirt and pantyhose, glad I didn't wear jeans, as I say, "Thank you."

The server comes to pour two glasses of what I assume is champagne before leaving the room and shutting the door behind him.

I turn my attention to Dario and catch him staring at me.

Suddenly feeling awkward, I mutter, "Sooo…here we are."

A sexy grin curves the corner of his mouth. "Here we are."

"Have you eaten here before?" I ask to make conversation.

He nods as he answers, "My friend is the owner. She's also one of the best chefs, so prepare yourself for an award-winning meal." He pauses for a moment before saying, "I hope you don't mind, but I already placed the order for the signature dish."

"Oh…I don't mind."

God, I hope it isn't prawns or some kind of shellfish. That shit gives me the creeps.

"What did you do yesterday?" he asks.

"I worked." I can see he wants to ask what I do for a living, so I add, "I'm a waitress at a diner."

"Is it one of those that's open twenty-four-seven?" he asks.

Shit. Friday night, I told him I had to get back to work, which is probably why he's asking the question.

Hating that I have to lie, I nod.

There's a pause in the conversation, then Dario says, "Tell me about yourself."

And just like that, I hit a blank. I can't come up with something interesting to say, so I ask, "What do you want to know?"

"Do you have siblings? What's your family dynamic like?"

Letting out a chuckle, I pick up the glass and take a sip of the bubbly liquid that's the best alcohol I've ever tasted.

"Wow. This tastes good."

"I'm going to assume by the chuckle that you feel uncomfortable talking about your family."

"Yeah. It's not my favorite topic." I take another sip, then say, "I have no idea who my father is and my mother…let's just say we don't get along at all."

My tongue darts out to collect the drops on my lips, then I ask, "What about you?"

Dario inhales deeply, then says, "I lost my parents at a young age."

"I'm sorry," I murmur. "Do you have any other family?"

He nods, but not telling me about them, he changes the subject by asking, "Have you always loved dancing?"

I shrug as I think about how to answer him.

"It's a nice hobby that helps me deal with stress."

"Just a hobby? Why didn't you pursue a career as a dancer?"

"God, I could never do that. I've seen the pressure the ballerinas are under. That shit's not for me. I've only danced in front of two people. My neighbor…and you."

A frown instantly forms on his forehead. "Your neighbor?"

A soft smile spreads over my face. "Tyrone. He's like a father to me."

Memories of the past pop into my head, drawing a happy chuckle from me.

"When I was younger, I used to put on little shows for him, and he would cheer and clap as if it was the best performance he's ever seen."

The door opens, and the conversation is paused while the server brings in our food.

So far, the date is going better than I expected. Hopefully, I don't screw things up because I'm enjoying it.

Chapter 12

Dario

When the server leaves the room again, I say, "It's spicy Korean brisket." There's a relieved expression on Eden's face that has me asking, "Were you worried it would be something else?"

"Yeah, I don't eat shellfish. They're like the roaches of the ocean."

I've interacted with hundreds of women, and none of them are as straightforward as Eden. It's like she doesn't care about what she says or who's there to hear it. It's refreshing.

When I pick up my chopsticks and spoon, Eden watches me take a bite before she grabs her fork and says, "I've never eaten with those things, and I'm not about to start."

Wanting her to feel comfortable, I swap my chopsticks for a fork, earning a smile from her.

Resuming the conversation, I say, "Tell me more about Tyrone."

"Oh, I've known him since forever. We look out for each other."

"I'm glad you have someone who cares about you," I mention. Wanting to know more about her, I ask, "Do you live close to the ballet company?"

Her features tense as she shakes her head, then she exhales a sigh and says, "I live on the other side of the city."

Feeling like she's hiding something from me, I murmur, "We've had sex, *Tesoro*. I think it's safe for you to tell me where you live."

A frown line forms between her eyes. "Is that Italian?" When I nod, she asks, "What does it mean?"

"The direct translation is treasure, but it can also be used for sweetheart."

"Oh."

She takes hold of her glass and twirls it on the white tablecloth, giving me the impression she's feeling awkward again.

Her eyes flick to mine before focusing on the bubbles in her champagne.

"Which one do you mean when you say it?"

I wait until her eyes flick to mine again, then answer, "Both."

I watch as she takes two sips of the expensive drink. She clears her throat, and picking up her fork, she focuses too much attention on her meal.

Suddenly, she pins me with a serious expression. "Why did you ask me on a date?"

"Why not?"

She drops the fork in the bowl, and straightening her spine, it looks like she's getting ready for a fight.

"We come from different worlds," she states the obvious. "Honestly, it's the first time I'm in a nice place like this. It's obvious you're used to expensive things."

I shrug and tilt my head. "Your point being?"

"You're rich, and I'm not."

I stare at her for a long moment, realizing money is a big issue for her.

My tone is soft as I say, "It's not a problem for me."

She gives me a mocking look. "Yeah, until you find out where I live." Her shoulders slump slightly, then she says, "Look, the sex was great, and I've enjoyed hanging out with you, but I don't see this going anywhere."

Feeling tense, I mutter, "I think you're wrong. As you said, the sex was great. That alone is a reason to keep seeing each other."

"I'm not going to be your fuck buddy."

"I don't take my fuck buddies on dates."

She rubs her palm over her forehead, looking frustrated, then she suddenly admits, "I live in Brownsville."

Christ.

It's impossible for me to hide the shock at hearing she lives in one of the most dangerous neighborhoods in New York. Brownsville is a fucking thorn in the Cosa Nostra's side with all the drug dealers and gangs running rampant in the area.

"See. I was right." Eden misinterprets my reaction. "Rich people like you will always look down on the poor."

Standing up, she walks to where her coat is hanging.

A coat that's so fucking worn it can't possibly keep her warm.

"I'm shocked because you live in a dangerous area," I explain. "Sit down." She hesitates, which has me adding, "Please."

Eden looks visibly upset as she takes a seat again, and I wait for her to meet my eyes before I say, "I don't care whether you're poor or rich, but hearing you live in such a dangerous place, where drug dealers and gangs are out of control, worries the fuck out of me."

Her shoulders hunch forward. "It's home and not all bad."

She's living in a fucking war zone, but if I make an issue out of it, she's going to walk out of here, and I'll never see her again.

Fuck.

She leans a little forward in her seat. "Most of my neighbors are hard-working people. We look out for each other." She stares at me for a moment, then says, "If it's something that's going to bother you, then it's best we end things now."

Knowing she has people looking out for her makes me feel better, but I need to get the word out in Brownsville that no one's to lay a finger on her.

"It doesn't bother me," I say to put her at ease.

When I resume eating, Eden clears her throat. "I tend to get defensive about my circumstances."

I let out a chuckle. "I've noticed."

"I don't expect anything from you," she blurts out. When I glance at her, she explains, "Like…stuff. I don't need you buying me shit to win me over. I'm here because I like you."

She likes me. It's a start.

When I nod, she adds, "And the sex is good."

Laughter escapes from me, which eases the tension in the air. "Eat your food so I can take you home, and we can check whether the great sex was a one-time thing."

"I'm warning you now, you and your sports car are going to stand out like a sore thumb."

Every drug dealer and gang member knows who I am, and they won't dare fuck with me.

"I can handle it," I murmur.

We eat for a while longer before Eden asks, "Do you enjoy what you do?" Her tongue darts out to lick her lips then she adds, "Working with ballerinas."

"I love it." Wanting her to know a little more about me, I say, "I also own an opera house."

She's quiet for a moment, then asks, "So you're Italian?"

"Sicilian," I correct her.

When we're done eating, Eden says, "Thank you for dinner. It was delicious."

"I'll tell Skylar you loved it."

"Is that your chef-friend's name?"

"Yes."

Standing up, I walk to where Eden's coat is hanging, and taking it off the hook, I hold it open so she can push her arms through the sleeves.

I move my hands to her shoulders and turn her around so she'll face me. Staring into her gray eyes, I slowly lower my head and press a tender kiss to her lips.

I can't pinpoint what it is about her, but the more time I get to spend with her, the more I want to be around her.

Pulling back, I say, "I like you too, *Tesoro*."

Taking hold of her hand, I weave our fingers together before we leave the room.

When we weave through the tables toward the exit, Renzo comes in, and the instant his eyes lock on Eden and me, his eyebrows fly up into his hairline.

Here we go.

His focus shifts to Eden, and only when we reach him does he meet my eyes.

"Hey," I say. "Renzo, this is Eden." Tugging her closer to me, I explain, "She's the dancer I told you about."

A smile forms on Eden's face, and she holds her free hand out to him. "It's nice to meet you. Are you a friend of Dario's?"

"I'm his best friend," Renzo chuckles.

I watch as he shakes her hand, and when they're done, I tell him, "I'll call you later."

"Okay." A smile that spells nothing good for me forms on his face. "Have fun."

I teased Renzo and Franco endlessly when they met their women and fell in love. There's no way they'll miss a chance to get back at me.

Leaving the restaurant, Eden says, "I had a nice time. Thank you."

I glance down at her as I lead her to where I parked my SUV, which I'm using because Bella peed on the passenger seat of my R8, so I've had it sent to be cleaned.

When I open the passenger door, Eden chuckles, "In case you missed it, that was me giving you a chance to back out of taking me home."

"I'm not backing out." I nod my head toward the car, encouraging her to get in.

Once she climbed into the passenger side, I shut the door and walk around the SUV.

As I slide behind the steering wheel, I say, "Seat belt, *Tesoro*."

She pulls on the seat belt, then asks, "Are you fluent in Italian?"

"Yes." I start the engine and check for traffic before I pull away from the curb.

"Oooh. Tell me something dirty in Italian."

I think for a moment, and lowering my voice to a seductive tone, I say, "*Adoro il modo in cui si sente la tua figa attorno al mio cazzo.*"

She places her hand on my thigh and moves it dangerously close to where my cock is growing hard.

"What does it mean?"

"I love the way your pussy feels around my cock."

She lets out an unexpected snort that's followed by laughter. "Sorry. Even though I knew you would say something like that, it still caught me off guard."

"You're not used to men talking dirty to you?" I ask, and as soon as the question is out, I really want to hear the answer.

"No." She gives my thigh a squeeze. "You make it sound hot."

I stop the SUV at a red light then capture her eyes with mine. "Does it turn you on?" She nods, which has me asking, "What else turns you on?"

She shrugs and thinks for a moment. "Spontaneous hot sex. The kind where clothes are ripped off and furniture is broken."

The corner of my mouth lifts in a smirk as I mutter, "I like the sound of that."

"What's a turn-on for you?" she asks.

"Everything you did on Friday night."

A wide smile spreads over her face. "Unfortunately for you, that was a one-time performance."

"I'll just have to cherish it then."

When I enter Brownsville, Eden gives me her address.

People instantly take notice of my arrival, and as I steer the SUV toward the apartment block where Eden lives, I see one scout after another making calls to notify their gang members that I'm here.

No one will risk a thing while I'm in the neighborhood because they don't want to get into shit with the Cosa Nostra.

"You can park there, where the group of people are sitting on the sidewalk," Eden says.

I bring the SUV to a standstill, and when we get out, an African-American man who looks like he's in his early fifties gets up from the plastic chair he's occupying. He reminds me of the actor in *The Green Mile*.

His eyes dart from Eden to me.

"Is this your date, baby girl?" he asks Eden, a wave of protectiveness coming off him.

Eden walks closer and give him a kiss on the cheek. "Yes. Be nice, Tyrone."

"I'll be nice as long as he doesn't give me a reason to be otherwise," Tyrone says.

I like this man.

Holding my hand out to him, I treat Tyrone the same way I would any father of a girl I'm interested in. "It's nice to meet you, sir."

"None of that *sir* shit. Tyrone's just fine."

His eyes snap to our left, and he stares at a black sedan that's slowly creeping up the street.

I glance in the direction of the vehicle and notice it's Frankie, a gangster whose main source of income is stealing cars. Four of his men are in the car with him.

They're in the midst of a territory war with another gang, and I'm actually rooting for Frankie to win.

"You just keep on driving by," Tyrone shouts. "Nothing to see here." Then he looks at Eden. "Get your man inside before someone tries to mug him for his expensive clothes."

Frankie gives me a chin lift before the sedan speeds away.

"Yeah," Tyrone calls after the car. "That's right. Drive away, motherfuckers."

"That's enough, Tyrone," Eden mutters. "Don't piss them off."

We walk into a building and head up the stairs to the third floor. When Tyrone follows us into the apartment, Eden says, "Don't give him shit."

"I'm just gonna lay out the law for him," he mutters before giving me a once-over. "What's your name?"

Fuck. There's a chance Tyrone might know about the Cosa Nostra.

"His name is Dario. He owns a ballet company. Don't ask more questions," Eden rambles, looking nervous. "I'll come over when he leaves and tell you everything about him."

"Ohhhh," Tyrone says, sounding as if he's just realized something. The next second, he gives me a wide, toothy smile. "It was nice meeting you." He walks to the door. "I'll keep an eye on your car so no one jacks your wheels."

"Thanks," I murmur. When he shuts the door behind him, I turn to face Eden. "Did I miss something?"

"No. Tyrone's just weird like that." She shrugs off her coat. "You want something to drink? I have juice and coffee."

I glance around the small space. "No, thanks. I'm good."

Shock hits me square in the gut when I take in the shitty apartment Eden calls home.

There's an old-as-fuck couch and a coffee table that's missing a leg. A stack of bricks keeps it from tipping over.

The walls haven't seen a fresh coat of paint in the last decade or two, and it looks like the windows are nailed shut.

I'm struggling to process Eden's circumstances, which are nothing short of horrific and the complete opposite of mine.

Doing my best to hide my reaction, I turn my attention back to her, and seeing how she's watching me, I smile and say, "We're alone."

"We are." Her lips curve up. "What do you want to do?"

"We can sit and talk."

The smile drops from her face. "Talk? I thought you wanted to have sex?"

Taking her hand, I pull her to the couch and take a seat beside her. "That can wait. Let's get to know each other better."

"Oh…okay."

She turns her body, and resting her shoulder against the back of the couch, she looks at me. "You said Renzo is one of your best friends. Do you have a lot of friends?"

I nod. "And you?"

"I have a few. I'm close with another waitress."

Lifting my arm around her shoulders, I tug her closer until she's leaning into me, and for the next hour, we talk about safe topics.

Chapter 13

Dario

"Where's the restroom?" I ask.

Eden pulls away from me and points to a closed door. "Over there."

I get up and walk the short distance. When I open the door, I glance into a bedroom where I see a neatly made bed with pink covers and pillows.

Going into the restroom, I shut the door and relieve my bladder. While I wash my hands, I notice a laundry hamper with the tight shorts and shirt Eden was wearing Friday night.

Remembering the great sex, I start to get hard, but I adjust my cock into a more comfortable position, then ignore the thing because I don't plan on fucking Eden tonight.

Glancing around, I notice there's only a shower, a toilet, and a small sink. The single cupboard above the sink is packed with toiletries. The toothpaste is squeezed empty. There can't possibly be anything left in the tube.

It keeps hitting me how poor Eden is, and everything in me screams to help her. However, I get the feeling if I tried to help out, she'd lose her shit, and that would be the end of us.

I'll just have to be patient until we're an actual item.

Stepping out of the restroom, I return to the couch and sit down again.

My eyes drift over Eden's face as I wrap my arm around her shoulders, wishing I could take her out of this place.

Patience, Dario.

She snuggles into my side, and brushing her palm over my *Balenciaga* sweater, she asks, "Why do you like to watch me dance?"

"It calms me," I answer honestly. "There's something about your movements that casts a spell over me."

She tilts her head back to look up at me, and we stare at each other for a moment before I say, "I love looking at you."

"Ditto."

I lower my head and slowly press my mouth to hers. When she tries to deepen the kiss, I lift my hand to her face and grip hold of her jaw to keep her in place. I keep the pace slow, taking my time exploring her mouth and memorizing her taste.

Eden grows impatient and tries to move onto my lap, but in a swift move, I pin her down on the couch, and locking my fingers around her throat, I force her to take it slow as I continue to kiss her tenderly.

Her breaths become shaky, and her fingers dig harder and harder into my biceps as my tongue caresses hers as if she's my greatest treasure.

When I finally free her mouth and lift my head, Eden's eyes slowly flutter open, and she stares up at me as if I've performed some kind of miracle.

She looks at me as if I'm a god, and it makes me close the distance between us so I can continue worshiping her mouth.

I have no idea how long we kiss, and I love every second, but the apartment's getting colder and colder with each passing minute.

When the place feels like a fucking freezer, I lift my head and scowl down at Eden. "Does it always get this cold in here?"

"No. I think the heat went out again." She gives me an apologetic look. "Coffee?"

The corner of my mouth lifts, and I press another soft kiss to her lips before I sit up. "That would be nice."

Eden gets up, and going to the kitchen, she makes two cups of coffee. She adds one sugar to mine and three to hers before she brings the cups to the living room.

"Thanks," I murmur as I take the beverage from her.

She sits down again and tucks one of her legs beneath her. Getting comfortable, she sips on her coffee while she stares at me.

"Does the heat go out often?" I ask, worried about her sleeping in the cold.

"Yeah, but I have extra blankets, so don't worry. I'll get the building manager to fix it tomorrow."

Hearing that makes me feel better.

We're quiet for a moment before she says, "It's weird."

"What?"

"Even though you're into ballet and opera, it feels as if there's something edgy about you that I can't quite place my finger on." Her foot rubs up and down my shin, as she admits, "It has a weird pulling effect on me. It makes me want to dig beneath all the expensive clothes to see what you're hiding." Looking at me from over the rim of her cup, she murmurs, "Do you have a dark side, Dario?"

You have no idea, Tesoro. I have a long list of bodies lying in my wake, but that's a conversation for another time.

Bringing my hand to her face, I trail my fingers along the sexy curve of her jaw. "Everyone has a dark side."

She finishes the last of her coffee and sets the cup down on the rickety coffee table before she snuggles against my side again.

After a few minutes of silence, she asks, "Do you really want to date someone like me?"

I don't hesitate to answer, "Yes."

She tilts her head back to meet my eyes. "Do you think it could work between us?"

I nod. "Definitely."

Her gaze searches mine for something. "Are you going to break my heart?"

I set my coffee down so I can place my hand against her cheek, and giving her an earnest look, I promise, "I'll never hurt you intentionally."

She pushes closer to me until I can feel her breath warming my lips. "Where do we go from here?"

"We date," I murmur before brushing my mouth against hers. "No seeing other people. I don't share."

"I don't share either," she whispers as she crawls onto my lap. "If you cheat on me, I'll key your sports car."

I let out a burst of laughter. "Luckily for my car, I'm a one-woman-at-a-time man."

"Good." She presses kisses along my jaw and down my throat, then whispers against my skin, "You smell so good."

I wrap my arms around her and squash her to my chest as my mouth finds hers. Again, I have to restrain her so I can kiss her deeply.

Lifting my head, I ask, "Have you never just made out with a guy?"

She lets out a chuckle. "That's so old school. No one does that anymore."

"I do." My eyes caress her beautiful face. "I love just kissing."

"Talking about old school. How old are you?" she asks.

"Thirty-one. You?"

"I'm not nearly as old as you," she says with a teasing tone. "I'm twenty-four."

My phone starts ringing, and it has Eden moving off my lap. I dig the device out, and seeing Franco's name so late at night, I say, "I have to take the call."

"Okay."

I get up and answer, "What's up?"

"Renzo says you're seeing someone. Why am I the last to find out?" he mutters.

"It's still brand new. I was going to tell you the next time I saw you."

"What's her name?"

"Eden..." I pause, my eyes flying to her as I realize I don't know her last name.

"What's your last name?" I ask.

She frowns at me. "Who wants to know?"

"I'm on a date," I tell Franco. "I'll call you when I'm done."

"Come over for a drink."

"Okay."

I end the call then focus my attention on Eden. "So, what's your last name?"

"Taylor." She gestures with her chin at my phone. "Who were you talking to?"

"One of my friends."

"Oh."

Walking closer, I lean over her and press a kiss to her mouth. "I'm going to head out. It's late, and you probably need to get some sleep."

"Yeah." She gets up off the couch and walks me to the door. "Thanks for this evening."

I press another kiss to her mouth. "You're welcome."

I leave the apartment and head down the stairs. When I exit the building, I immediately spot one of the local gang's scouts before he hurries around a corner.

I press the fob to unlock the SUV's doors and climb in. Starting the engine, I pull away from the curb, my eyes scanning the area as I slowly drive down the road. Not even a mile up, I see Frankie's black sedan. When I pull up behind him, he gets out while his friends remain in the car.

As he comes up beside my SUV, I let the window down.

"Mr. La Rosa," he says with respect coating his tone. "It's not every day we see you in these parts."

My eyes lock with his, and with the full force of the Cosa Nostra in my voice, I say, "If anything happens to Eden Taylor or her neighbor Tyrone, there will be hell to pay."

"She your girl?" he asks. When I nod, he says, "I'll spread the word."

"Want to make some money on the side?" I ask.

"I'm always looking for extra cash." He glances around us. "What you got in mind?"

"Keep her safe without her finding out I hired you."

He nods, his eyes constantly roaming the area for any threats. "Sure. I can do that."

When I start to let the window up, Frankie walks back to his sedan and gets in.

Frankie and his men wait for me to drive past before they follow me to the border of Brownsville. Flashing their lights, they make a U-turn, then head back the way they came.

Feeling better now that I have some kind of protection detail on Eden, I drive to Franco's place.

Chapter 14

Eden

When Dario leaves, I shut the door and lean against it.

Wow.

Lifting a hand to my face, I brush the tips of my fingers over my lips.

I've never been kissed like that.

Warmth spreads through my chest while there are flutters in my stomach.

I think it's safe to say I'm crushing hard on Dario, and if I'm not careful, I'll be head over heels in love before I know it.

Closing my eyes, I get lost in the memory of having his body pinning me down on the couch while his mouth did things to mine that had me almost crying with the emotions it stirred in my heart.

The man really has a way of making me feel special…as if I could be his entire world.

Don't be stupid.

My eyes snap open, and shaking my head, I open the door and head to Tyrone's place.

I knock quickly, and he opens within seconds with a grin on his face.

"So, you and your boss?"

"I almost had a panic attack when you started asking him questions!" I go inside where it's warmer. "Dario doesn't know I'm a janitor at his company."

A frown forms on Tyrone's brow. "Why?"

"Because I'm not ready for him to know." I sit down on his couch, then say, "The heat is out in my apartment."

"Want to crash here tonight?"

"No, I have the extra blanket. I'll tell Winston tomorrow so he can fix it."

Tyrone takes a seat on the armchair and pins me with a serious look. "So why aren't you ready for your boss to know you work for him?"

"Duh." I wave a hand in the air. "Show me a rich guy who wants to date a woman who cleans toilets and scrubs floors."

"There's nothing wrong with being a janitor," Tyrone mutters. "It's honest money."

"I know." I let out a sigh. "But what if he finds out and fires my ass?"

"Why would he fire you? You haven't done anything wrong."

"Yeah, I have. I steal half an hour of company time to dance in one of the studios."

"Just say you were doing it during a break. You're allowed to take breaks, right?"

"True." My teeth tug at my bottom lip, then I look at Tyrone. "I really like him."

A smile spreads over his face. "Yeah? You think he likes you too?"

Grinning like an idiot, I nod. "The way he kisses me makes me feel special."

"The man's got game." Tyrone raises an eyebrow at me. "Just make sure he wraps it before you-know-what."

I pull a grossed-out face. "Eww...don't give me the birds and bees talk."

Chuckling, he says, "You're the one who started talking about kissing. I just want to make sure my girl doesn't get knocked up."

Changing the subject back to a safer topic, I ask, "What do you think of Dario?"

Tyrone shakes his head. "I didn't get to spend time with him, so it's hard to say." He shrugs, then chuckles. "Either the man got one hell of a hard-on for you or he has a spine of steel. You know, with him coming here and all. He didn't seem worried for his safety."

"True," I murmur, thinking back to when we came home earlier.

Dario actually seemed relaxed, as if he'd been here a million times before.

"There was something else," Tyrone muses.

My eyes snap to his face. "What?"

"That motherfucker Frankie. Was it my imagination, or did he give us a chin lift on the drive-by?"

"I didn't see. I was too busy glaring at you for mouthing off at them. You need to stop doing that," I chastise him.

Tyrone grumbles something I can't make out, then gets up from the armchair. "You want some coffee or tea?"

"No, I just had coffee. Thanks, though." I get up as well. "I'm gonna go to bed. I'll see you tomorrow."

Tyrone starts to make a cup of tea for himself and glances at me. "Sweet dreams, baby girl."

"You too." I let myself out of his apartment and head back to my place.

Locking the front door behind me, I turn off the lights in the living room and walk to my bedroom to change into my warm PJs, which consist of my oldest sweatpants and a sweater.

I go to the bathroom and quickly wash my face before I fight the toothpaste tube for the last bit. I end up cutting the thing open and grin when I see there's enough for tomorrow morning.

I brush my teeth, and after I'm done, I dig my cell phone out of my coat's pocket and plug it in on my bedside table so it can charge overnight.

I switch off the rest of the lights and crawl beneath the blankets on my bed, snuggling into my pillow.

My thoughts are instantly consumed by Dario.

Today's date might have started rocky, but it ended up going much better than I expected.

Dario handled the news of where I live and seeing my apartment so well. I don't feel like he was judging me at all.

Can things really work out between us?

My heart beats faster at the thought of dating Dario. I mean, he's one hell of a catch.

Why me, though? Out of all the women he interacts with on a daily basis, why did he even spare me a second glance?

He could've picked any of the gorgeous ballerinas. Or whoever sings at the opera house he owns. Or one of the rich women in his social circle.

I was the one who was on a date with him today, though.

He kissed me.

If he were just in it for a quick fuck, I wouldn't have seen him today.

That means he's seriously interested in me.

A happy grin spreads over my mouth, and I giggle like a freaking schoolgirl.

Dario La Rosa likes me.

A banging on my front door rips me out of my thoughts, and letting out a sigh, I throw the covers back and climb out of bed.

I switch on the light, and while the banging increases until I'm sure the noise will wake all my neighbors, I shove my feet into my sneakers.

Leaving my bedroom, I rush to the front door and check through the peephole.

Jesus Christ.

Unlocking the door, I yank it open, and when Mandy tries to stagger inside, I shove her backward.

"No! Get out of here," I bark.

"Come on," she slurs. She's so drunk it's a miracle she's able to keep her balance. "Let your mamma in."

Tyrone's door opens, and when he sees Mandy, his features tighten with anger. "Enough, Mandy. Go find somewhere else to sleep."

"Shut up! Some of us are trying to sleep," Mrs. Wendall shouts from the end of the hallway.

"You shut up," Mandy yells back at her before she gives me a dazed smile. "I'm visiting my pretty daughter."

Having had enough, I grab hold of Mandy's arm and drag her down the stairs so I can throw her out of the building.

"Hey, hey, hey," she slurs while struggling to keep up with me. "Be a good kid and let your mamma crash on the couch. It's cold outside."

I pull Mandy out onto the sidewalk and almost have a heart attack when I see Junior, one of Frankie's men, parked in front of the entrance.

Shit.

Is he here because Tyrone mouthed off to Frankie?

Junior climbs out of his car and scowls at Mandy and me.

My stomach churns, and my muscles tense up with fear. Mandy, on the other hand, takes one look at the gangster, yanks free from my hold, then runs away like the coward she is.

Shivering from the cold, I wrap my arms around myself, while keeping my eyes on Junior.

Knowing words won't stop him, I still say, "We're not looking for any trouble."

"Just keeping the apartment safe," he mutters. "It's cold out here, ma'am. Go back inside."

What. The. Hell?

Did he just call me ma'am?

With my jaw dropped open, I stare at the dangerous gangster.

Stunned, I stumble over the single word. "W-why?"

"Just taking care of our people." He jerks his chin toward the entrance. "Go."

Since when does Frankie's gang care about 'our people'?

Confused as hell, I keep glancing at Junior as I walk back into the building. When I reach the third floor, Tyrone's still standing by his open door.

"So, something weird just happened," I say. "Junior is parked out front, saying he's keeping the place safe because he's," I make quotation marks in the air with my fingers, "Just taking care of our people."

A dark frown forms on Tyrone's forehead. "What are the motherfuckers up to?"

"Beats me." I walk to my front door. "Mandy took off running when she saw Junior. I don't think she'll risk coming back tonight."

"Thank you, Jesus, for small mercies," Tyrone mutters. He gives me a chin lift. "Go back to bed."

"Don't confront Junior," I say while giving him a serious look.

"Yeah-yeah."

I wait until Tyrone shuts his front door before I go back into my apartment. Locking up behind me, I rush back to bed and quickly kick off my sneakers. I dive beneath the covers and curl into a ball so I can warm up again.

Within seconds, my thoughts are consumed by Dario again, and with the memory of him kissing me, I drift off to sleep.

Chapter 15

Dario

When I walk into Franco's house, I hear one of the triplets crying. Following the sound, I find Franco in the living room, trying to soothe Augusto.

"Hey," I say, and smiling at the baby boy, I take him from Franco. "Aww…did you miss Uncle Dario." I rest him against my chest and press kisses to his head.

Augusto sticks his thumb into his mouth and starts to calm down.

"How the fuck do you do that?" Franco asks as he slumps down on one of the couches.

I take a seat, and leaning back, I press another kiss to Augusto's soft hair.

"I have the magic touch," I chuckle.

Within seconds, the little one falls asleep in my arms, earning me a thankful look from Franco.

"Tell me about the woman you're dating."

"It's only been one date," I say.

"You took her to Skylar's restaurant. It means you're serious," Franco states a fact I can't deny.

I take a minute to examine my feelings and gather my thoughts before I admit, "I like her a lot. She's different from other women."

Franco locks eyes with me. "Where did you meet?"

"I saw her dancing at the ballet company, and one thing led to another."

He lifts an eyebrow at me. "Oh, so she's a ballerina?"

I shake my head. "No, she's a waitress at a diner." A frown forms on my forehead. "I'm actually not sure what she was doing at the ballet company."

"And you didn't think to check into it?" He leans forward and rests his forearms on his knees. "Hacking and tracking is your job."

"I know." I shrug, then admit, "I don't want to invade her privacy. I want to get to know her like a normal person."

"I'm going to assume she doesn't know you're a part of the Cosa Nostra," he mutters.

I nod while rubbing my hand up and down Augusto's back.

"I'll tell her once we're an item."

Franco lets out a sigh. "Good luck with that. I almost lost Samantha when she found out."

Yeah. I have no idea how Eden will react to hearing I'm a mafia boss, but that's a problem for later in the relationship.

The corner of Franco's mouth lifts. "Have you slept with her?"

I glare at my friend. "I'm not telling you shit about my sex life."

He lets out a burst of laughter that has Augusto stirring in my arms.

"I'm taking that as a yes, which means you're more serious about the woman than you care to admit."

"I didn't say I wasn't serious about Eden."

We're quiet for a moment while I take a deep breath of Augusto's addictive baby scent, then I say, "I asked Frankie to keep an eye on Eden."

A dark frown forms on Franco's face as he asks, "Frankie, the gangster?"

"Yeah. Eden lives in Brownsville."

"Christ," my friend mutters. "Damiano just fucking declared war on Miguel's gang. Didn't you hear a thing he said at the meeting?"

"I'm well aware of what's happening in Brownsville, hense me asking Frankie to watch out for Eden."

"Why not just get her out of there?" he asks.

"Eden has one hell of an independent and defensive streak. If I push her, I'll lose her."

"Kidnap her."

"My kidnapping quota has been filled when I stole Bella earlier this week."

"Who the fuck is Bella?"

A grin spreads over my face as I dig my phone out of my pocket. "Come sit here so I can show you the photos."

When Franco takes a seat at my side, I open the gallery on my phone and scroll through photo after photo of Bella.

"A dog," Franco mutters. "You stole a dog?"

"Not just any dog. Isn't she the most adorable thing you've ever seen?"

"It's a dog, Dario."

I shoot my friend a glare. "She's not just any dog! She's my baby."

A photo of Bella sleeping in bed with me pops up, and I grin again. "Look how cute this one is. I could just eat her up."

Franco lets out a chuckle, and shaking his head, he reaches for Augusto. "Let me put him in bed."

"I'm going to hit the road," I say while climbing to my feet.

"Thanks for stopping by."

I let myself out of the house, and once I'm behind the steering wheel of my SUV, my thoughts turn to Eden.

I learned a lot about her today. Even though she's a fighter, she also craves love. The way she looked at me when I kissed her told me as much.

Fuck. I loved kissing her.

Thinking about her dire circumstances, has my jaw clenching and my fists tightening around the steering wheel.

With a snap of my fingers, I can change her entire life, but I know she'll fight me on it. Eden doesn't come across as the type of person who'll willingly accept handouts.

Inspecting my feelings, I think it's safe to say I care about her. She's got a hold on me, I can't shake.

At the rate things are progressing between us, it's only a matter of time before I fall completely in love with her.

After I park the SUV in the basement, I take the elevator up to my apartment. When the doors slide open, Bella lets out a bark, and a second later, she comes running toward me with her entire backside wiggling from excitement.

I scoop her up and let her lick my jaw as I say, "Did you miss Daddy?"

Esmerelda gets up from where she's watching TV, and I smile at her. "Thanks for babysitting."

She comes to rub Bella's head. "She was so good. She nudged me with her nose every time she needed to go out."

"Aww…"

"She should be fine for the rest of the night," Esmerelda says as she presses the button for the elevator.

"See you tomorrow."

Esmerelda takes the elevator down to the fifth floor, where her apartment is. I have another apartment on that floor, which I purchased as an investment, but I never got a tenant for it. It's something I'll get around to when I have some spare time.

I switch off all the lights, and head to my bedroom with Bella in my arms, while thinking Esmerelda's been with me through thick and thin.

She's more like family, especially after my parents died in a fire that almost killed me as well. Esmerelda woke up in time and managed to get us out, but my parents weren't so lucky.

I place Bella on the bed before grabbing a pair of sweatpants. When I head into the bathroom, she comes after me.

While I shower, Bella lies down on the pile of clothes I left on the floor.

I love how she follows me everywhere.

"You're glad I stole you, right?" I ask her.

She lifts her head and just looks at me for a moment before going back to sleep.

When I'm done in the bathroom, I climb into bed and hold the covers up so Bella can crawl beneath them. She presses against my side and rests her head on my chest before instantly falling asleep again.

"I wish I could fall asleep as quickly as you," I mutter as I shove an arm beneath my head.

Staring up at the ceiling, my thoughts go back to Eden, and I think of how my beautiful dancer is creeping into my heart.

Grabbing my phone, I unlock the screen and type out a message.

Dario: I want to see you again. Don't make me wait a whole week.

Knowing she might be asleep, I set the device down and close my eyes.

If Eden tells me she can only meet me on Sundays, I'm not going to be happy.

There's a burst of exhilaration in my chest as I realize I want to see her every single second of every day.

Christ. I've already fallen for her.

Chapter 16

Eden

I haven't been able to stop thinking about Dario all day. I even agreed to meet him for a quick cup of coffee a couple of blocks away from the ballet company, which means I haven't had time to eat dinner.

I have the burger I got from the diner in the secondhand bag, which I bought at a thrift store earlier. I'll eat it during my shift at work.

I walk to Half & Half, the coffee shop where I'm meeting Dario, and as soon as I enter the establishment, I spot him sitting at a corner table with his back to the wall.

He instantly notices me and stands up. When I'm close enough, he pulls me into a tight-as-hell hug, which I love.

Holding each other for a moment, I soak in the warmth coming from his body and the feel of his arms around me.

Yep, I've got it bad for this man.

He pulls back and presses a kiss to my mouth before he smiles at me, his eyes roaming over my face.

"I missed you."

"You saw me yesterday," I chuckle as we let go of each other and take our seats.

"Yeah, but that was hours ago," he complains. "I wish you didn't have to go to work. I need more than ten minutes of your time."

My stomach grumbles loudly, which has Dario's eyes snapping to my waist. "Are you hungry?"

I wave a hand in the air. "I'll eat when I get to work."

There's a rough edge to his tone when he asks, "What have you eaten today?"

Something tells me I'll be late for work if I admit I haven't had time to eat all day. This morning, I was busy with Winston, who fixed the heating in my apartment, and the shift at the diner was so crazy I didn't even get to drink something.

Lying, I say, "I had a big lunch. Stop worrying."

"What can I get you?" Dario asks as he stands up again.

"A hot chocolate, please."

"Be right back."

I watch him walk to the counter and take in the light blue suit he's wearing today. The color suits him, and he looks way too attractive.

I glance at the other tables and notice how women take notice of him, and it makes jealousy bleed into my chest.

When Dario's done placing our order, he glances at me, and the corner of his mouth lifts in a sexy grin.

He keeps staring at me until the barista tells him the order is ready, and as he brings our beverages to the table, it starts to sink in that Dario is *really* interested in me.

He sets the steaming mug down in front of me, and moving his chair closer to mine, he sits down.

"Hi," I whisper.

He lifts his hand and brushes the back of his knuckles over my cheek before wrapping his hand around the side of my neck and leaning in for another kiss.

Against my lips, he murmurs, "Hi."

When he pulls back, and our eyes meet, I fall a little more for him. If we weren't in public, I'd be on his lap in a flash.

Dario tilts his head, and with a tender expression on his face, he asks, "What's that look for?"

"I'm trying not to fall head over heels for you," I admit.

A mischievous grin spreads over his face. "I'll have to up my game to make sure that happens."

"You up your game anymore, and I might just propose to you," I joke.

"Yeah." Leaning in, he steals another kiss. "As much as I want to beg you to take off from work, I know you have to go, so drink your hot chocolate. I'll drop you off at the diner so we can spend a couple of minutes longer together."

Shit.

My mind races to come up with a valid excuse as to why Dario can't take me to work.

"Ah...it's not far. I'll walk."

"Then I'll walk with you," Dario offers.

The only diner in our near vicinity is in the opposite direction of the ballet company, and it would be too risky. What if Dario decides to surprise me at the diner only to find out I don't work there?

Shit.

What do I do?

His eyes narrow on my face. "Or not? Do you have a problem with me taking you to work?"

It's on the tip of my tongue to spill the truth to him, but I'm too scared. What if it's something he can't get past? What if he has a policy that he doesn't date employees?

What if he fires me for fucking him while I was supposed to be working?

And then there's all the hours I've stolen to dance in the studio to also keep in mind.

I chicken out at the last second and say, "You need to get to the ballet company. I know you're very busy with the upcoming show. Besides, I'm going to call a friend and catch up with her on the way to work."

I can see Dario's not happy with the poor excuse, but luckily, he doesn't push the subject.

I take a couple of sips of my beverage before I press a quick kiss to the corner of his mouth.

Getting up, I say, "Good luck at work."

As I turn around to leave, Dario grabs hold of my hand and rises to his full height.

"Are you upset because I offered to take you to work?"

I quickly shake my head. "Of course not."

"Then what's wrong?"

I move closer to him, and smiling, I press a decent kiss to his mouth before saying, "Nothing's wrong. Call me when you're done with rehearsals?"

He nods, and when I pull my hand free, he lets me go.

When I'm out of the coffee shop, I rush to the corner and glance over my shoulder. Not seeing Dario, I quickly break out into a run toward the ballet company.

My heart is a thundering mess in my chest and my lungs are on fire as I dart past Quincy's desk, barely able to call out, "Hi."

"What's the hurry?" he shouts after me, but I don't waste time to stop and answer him.

Dario can be here any second.

Only when I reach the safety of the locker room, do I drop my bag on the floor and suck in desperate breaths of air.

Jesus.

Using the back of my hand, I wipe the sweat from my forehead before drinking some water straight from the faucet. I put on my apron and cap and hurry to where the supplies are kept.

Knowing everyone will be in the auditorium, I retrieve my cleaning cart and push it toward the offices.

When I'm done with Mrs. Stafford's office, I move to the next one. It's only then that I realize it must be the one Dario uses.

As I polish the wooden desk, I glance around, but I don't see anything to confirm it's Dario's.

I've just finished mopping the floor, and when I push the cart toward the door, it suddenly opens.

Dario walks in with his phone pressed to his ear. "Give me a week, and I'll find out everything about the group."

My heart almost jumps out of my chest. I duck my head low and push the cart so damn fast out of the office, praying Dario doesn't recognize my clothes under the apron.

I need to bring an extra set of clothes to wear at work.

Before the door shuts, I hear him say, "It will cost a hundred thousand. The regular price."

My eyebrows fly up as I move down the hallway in the direction of the studios.

Jesus, that's a lot of money. It will last me a lifetime and then some.

Wondering what could cost so much, I continue working while being extra careful not to cross paths with Dario again for the rest of the night.

Chapter 17

Dario

Eden and I have been dating for two weeks, and I'm starting to lose my patience because I don't get to see her as often as I'd like.

I've convinced her to spend the night at my place, and as I park the R8 in my designated spot, I can feel she's a little nervous.

The opening show is on Wednesday, and it will run straight through next weekend, which means I won't get to see Eden much with our conflicting schedules.

I grab her overnight bag from where it's lying by her feet and say, "Let's head up."

Climbing out of the car, I wait for Eden, and taking her hand, I lead her to the elevator.

"You don't live far from the ballet company," she mentions.

The elevator doors open, and we step inside. I scan my keycard for the top floor, then glance at her.

"Thank you for agreeing to spend the night with me."

She leans into my side and smiles up at me. "You're welcome."

When the doors open, Bella barks and comes barreling toward us.

"Oh my God!" Eden exclaims as she rips her hand from mine. She crouches in front of Bella. "I didn't know you had a dog."

"Her name is Bella," I say as I walk toward the living room.

Eden pets Bella's head before she straightens up and glances around my apartment. The smile drops from her face, and her lips part with shock.

"Holy shit," she whispers, her eyes wide as saucers.

She remains rooted to the spot by the elevators, her features drawn tight as she takes in the art on the walls, the expensive furniture, and the wide-open space.

Tension starts to build in the air, then she suddenly lets out a burst of laughter.

"Jesus, I'm too scared to move. I don't want to get dirt on the floor from my boots."

She brushes a shaky hand through her hair, and knowing she's completely overwhelmed by my wealth, I walk to her and take hold of her hand. I pull her to the living room and tug her down on the couch next to me.

She's still nervous as fuck as she says, "You have a stunning place. It's...it's."

"You're home," Esmerelda suddenly says as she appears from the direction of the kitchen.

Eden shoots to her feet. "Hi."

Esmerelda knows about Eden spending the night, so she doesn't look surprised as she says, "Hi. I'm Dario's housekeeper, Esmerelda. Please let me know if I can get you anything."

"It's nice to meet you, ma'am. Thank you. I'm okay. Thank you."

I grab her hand again and tug her back down onto the couch.

"You can go, Esmerelda. See you tomorrow."

Eden watches my housekeeper leave, then she glances around the apartment before she says, "I knew you had money, but this is insane. It really puts shit into perspective."

I keep my tone soft as I ask, "What shit?"

Eden waves a hand over the TV that covers half the wall and the leather couches.

She stands up again and walks to a life-size marble statue of a ballerina. It's a recently acquired piece, and I'm having two more made to put on either side of the elevator doors.

She almost touches the statue but shoves her hand behind her as if she's scared she might break it accidentally.

Turning her head, her eyes only meet mine for a second before she glances away again.

"We live in completely different worlds."

"It doesn't matter," I assure her. "At least not to me."

Eden walks to where Bella is lying on one of the other couches and avoids me by giving my dog attention.

"Eden," I murmur.

"Yeah?"

"Look at me."

She keeps brushing her hand over Bella while she glances at me.

"It doesn't matter to me," I say again.

She stares at me for a moment, then admits, "It matters to me." Letting out a mixture between a scoff and a chuckle, she looks at Bella again. "You're this perfect guy who has this perfect life, and I'm–" She shakes her head, and it makes worry creep into my heart.

"I'm far from perfect."

I'm a fucking mafia boss who has killed and who will kill again. If anything, Eden is too good for me.

She lifts her head again, and when she meets my eyes, she asks, "Why me?"

I get up, and closing the distance between us, I pull her off the couch and against my chest. I lock my arms around her and wait until she tilts her head back to look at me.

It might be way too soon, but it doesn't stop me from saying, "I'm starting to fall in love with you because you're a fighter who dances like an angel. You might not have much, but you've worked hard to carve out a little space for yourself in this world. You could've given in to your circumstances, but you're working your ass off to rise above them. That shit takes so much fucking courage and determination, and it demands my respect."

I can see how much my words are affecting her when her chin starts to quiver.

Lowering my head, I press a tender kiss to her trembling lips.

"I should be the one asking why me," I murmur while looking deep into her eyes. "What makes me so special that someone as amazing as you will look twice at me?"

Eden's breaths speed up as she keeps staring at me, then the next moment, her arms wrap around my neck, and her mouth slams into mine.

Grabbing hold of her ass, I lift her body against mine until she hooks her legs around my waist.

We kiss the fuck out of each other as I try to make it to the stairs. Giving up, I stop near a wall, and grabbing hold of her sweater, I yank the fabric over her head.

She lowers her legs, and we keep kissing while tearing off each other's clothes.

When we're finally naked, I grip her hip and shove her back against the wall. My eyes drift down her body, taking in the sight of her breasts and her pussy.

"Christ," I whisper. "You're fucking perfect."

Her fingers wrap around my hard-as-fuck cock, and she starts stroking me while peppering kisses all over my chest.

Her breath fans over my skin as she says, "You look so good I want to eat you."

With bated breath, I watch as Eden sinks to her knees, and when she sucks my cock into her mouth, I let out a pleasure-filled groan.

Never has anything looked so beautiful and sexy as the woman in front of me when she sucks me deep into her mouth.

"*Tesoro*," I say, already breathless from how amazing it feels. "I'm not going to last long."

Her eyes fill with so much seduction as she sucks me harder and harder, and soon I'm hit with an intense wave of pleasure as I come in her mouth.

Watching her swallow my cum before she licks her lips as if it's the best thing she's ever tasted has me yanking her off the floor.

Carrying her over my shoulder, I take the stairs two at a time in my hurry to get her to my bedroom.

Eden lets out a chuckle, which turns into a hiccup when I throw her down on the bed.

Grabbing hold of her knees, I shove her legs open wide. A second later, my mouth latches onto her soaked pussy with a hunger I can't control.

"Jesus," she gasps as her hand finds my hair. "I'm so glad I showered before you picked me up. Oh God. Oh. My. Godddd. Dario," she chants as I suck her clit and lap at her entrance like a starving man.

Her hips buck and gyrate with desperation, and I use my tongue and lips to push her over the edge.

Eden's body strains, and her ass lifts off the bed. Suspended in ecstacy, she doesn't breathe for a few seconds before she starts to convulse, and soft whimpers escape her lips. The erotic sight has me growing hard at the speed of light.

I swipe my tongue through her pussy before I press kisses over her abdomen and breasts as I crawl up her body. I suck a tight nipple into my mouth and scrape my teeth over her skin before pinning her body to my bed with my full weight.

Lying naked on top of her, I stare into her dazed eyes and watch as her pleasure fades.

I brush my hand up and down her side before slipping it beneath her thigh and lifting her leg over my ass so my cock can settle against her hot pussy.

She wraps her arms around my neck, and pressing her mouth to mine, her tongue brushes against mine.

I keep the kiss slow and deep, reveling in how good her naked body feels beneath me.

Minutes pass before I begin to stroke her pussy with my cock. Our breaths speed up, and our hands roam over each other's bodies.

When it feels like I'm going to explode, I reach down between us and position my cock at her entrance. My eyes latch onto hers, and with a single hard thrust, I bury myself all the way inside her.

Eden gasps, and if I weren't staring at her, I would've missed the flash of pain.

"You okay?" I ask.

She nods while a sexy smile pulls at her swollen lips. "Yes. I love how big you are. I can feel every inch of you inside me."

"Christ," I mutter before my mouth crashes against hers as I thrust even harder inside her.

"God, yes. Yes. Yes. Yes," she chants, and it has me moving into a kneeling position between her thighs.

I grip her ass with both my hands, and knowing she's able to handle me, I fuck her as rough as I want.

The muscles in my body strain as I keep slamming into her. Eden keeps her eyes on my face as she grabs hold of the covers while her back arches.

"Fuck," she cries, her features tightening. "Fuck me harder, baby."

Knowing exactly what she needs, I use my thumb to rub her clit hard, and within seconds, she lets out a broken cry as her body is seized by another orgasm.

I have to pull out, so I don't come yet, but I keep rubbing her clit, until she flinches from overstimulation.

Crawling over her body, I brace my hands on either side of her head. I stare down at her flushed cheeks and satisfied expression with pride.

When her breathing starts to slow down, she asks, "Did you come?"

I shake my head. "I'm not done making you come yet."

Her eyes widen. "What? I've had two orgasms. There's no way I'm coming again."

The corner of my mouth lifts. "I'm taking that as a challenge."

Moving back to make space, I flip her onto her stomach and use my body to push her down against the mattress.

"Oh, Jesus," she gasps.

Using my left hand, I pin her wrists above her head. I push her legs open with one of mine, while I trail a finger down the crack of her sexy ass.

I hear her suck in a deep breath, and when I drag the tip of my finger through her pussy, she jerks because she's still too sensitive.

I move my hand back to her ass cheek and massage her soft skin while I press kisses to her shoulder and neck.

"*Il tuo corpo è perfetto. Voglio scoparti tutta la notte,*" I say near her ear, my tone filled with need for her.

"Jesus, Dario," she moans as she pushes her ass into my palm. "That's so hot."

Positioning my cock at her entrance again, I enter her with short strokes, my hips rocking, and the sound of her slickness coating me loud in the air.

"Your body is perfect," I translate the words for her. "I want to fuck you all night long."

Pressing my chest against her back, I push my right hand beneath her until I'm able to squeeze her breast hard.

Eden's practically panting, and when I begin to fuck her torturously slowly, it sounds like she's sobbing while pleading, "Faster. I…need…more."

"I know," I growl near her ear as I keep the pace so fucking slow it's pushing me to my limits.

Pulling my hand free from beneath her, I pull out until only the head of my cock is inside her before I slap her ass.

I feel her pussy try to suck me deeper as a moan escapes my woman, followed by her croaking, "More."

As slowly as I can, I push back inside her, feeling every inch of her as she wraps around my cock. I smack her ass again, and then I have to fight to keep her still beneath me as she tries to move so she can increase the pace.

"Keep still, or I'm stopping," I warn her.

"That's mean," she whimpers.

I lean down and press a kiss to her jaw before I say, "Out in the world, you can be a badass independent woman, but in here, you'll submit to me."

"Yes, Mr. La Rosa."

Hearing the seductive as fuck words, my control slips, and I slam into her a few times before I'm able to regain enough control to slow my pace.

"Hmmm," she teases. "You liked that, didn't you?"

As an answer to her question, I smack her ass again.

I continue to torture both of us with painfully slow strokes until Eden's a gasping mess beneath me, whimpering incoherent words.

When I slam harder and harder into her, she instantly comes apart, hoarse cries the only sound she's able to make.

I fuck her until my own pleasure knocks the air from my lungs. My body slumps down on top of hers as intense ecstasy blinds me, rendering me completely helpless for a solid few minutes.

As the powerful orgasm begins to fade, my cock jerks inside her.

When we've both come down from the heights our pleasure took us to, I roll off her and focus on catching my breath.

Eden doesn't move a muscle as she mumbles, "I have zero strength."

I let out a chuckle, and throwing an arm around her, I press a kiss to her shoulder blade.

We enjoy the post-orgasm bliss for a while before I get up and walk to the bathroom. I grab a washcloth and wet it beneath warm water, then heading back in the room, I clean my woman's pussy while pressing more kisses over the length of her back.

When I'm done, I say, "Let's go downstairs so I can feed you."

Her head pops up, her hair all over the place. "Food sounds good."

I wait for her to crawl off the bed, and taking hold of her shoulders, I say, "Wait a second. Let me look at you."

She watches as I take my time looking at her beautiful body. I brush the tips of my fingers over her hard nipple and the curves of her hip.

"You're a work of art."

"The same could be said of you," she murmurs, her tone filled with happiness.

My eyes meet hers, and seeing the same look as when I kissed her on her couch – as if I performed some kind of miracle – I pull her into a hug and bury my face in her hair.

I won't take no for an answer. She will be mine.

No.

She is mine.

I'll give her the time she needs to get used to the idea of us, but after tonight, I'm never letting her go.

Chapter 18

Eden

Standing with the mop in my hand, I read the text Dario sent me a minute ago.

Can you take time off work to accompany me to the opening night?

I don't have anything fancy enough to wear to a ballet show, and people will recognize me.

Which means I have to tell Dario that I'm a janitor. After the amazing Sunday night we spent together, I don't think he'll fire me or break things off.

And I can scrounge up a few dollars to get a dress at a thrift store.

The corner of my mouth lifts as I type out a reply.

I'd love to. Can we meet up tomorrow morning? I need to tell you something.

I see he reads my message, then it shows he's typing.

Dario: 9 am at Half n Half?

Eden: Okay.

Suddenly, someone grabs hold of my shoulder and yanks me until I turn around.

"Where is it?" one of the ballerinas barks in my face.

"Where's what?"

"Don't play dumb. Where's my ring?"

The hell?

"Vivian, what's going on here," Mrs. Stafford asks as she comes down the hallway.

There's a sinking sensation in my stomach when I realize Vivian thinks I took her ring.

"The janitor stole my wedding ring," Vivian says, her voice trembling as she tries to fight back the tears.

"Let's go to my office," Mrs. Stafford orders. "The middle of the hallway is not the place for this discussion."

"But–" I start to argue, but Mrs. Stafford silences me with a stern look.

With a sigh, I place the mop back in my cart before I follow the women to the office. By the time Mrs. Stafford takes as seat behind her desk, anger is bubbling in my chest.

"I didn't take anything," I say, my voice tense.

"Pheobe said she saw the janitor in our dressing rooms during rehearsal," Vivian cries, visibly getting more and more upset with every passing second. "I left my wedding ring on the counter in my section."

Mrs. Stafford turns her attention to me, then asks, "Did you take it by accident? If you return the ring, we'll forget the whole unpleasant incident."

My temper flares, but I suck in a breath of air so I don't lose my cool. "I didn't take her ring."

Mrs. Stafford rises to her feet and comes to stand in front of me. The next moment, she shoves her hand into my apron's pocket and starts to search me.

I'm so offended my lips part with a gasp, and before I can stop myself, I smack her hand away from me. "Don't touch me!"

"See!" Vivian yells. "She's hiding something, or she would be fine with being searched."

"I didn't take your goddamn ring," I shout back at her.

Vivian's palm connects with my cheek, and I stagger a step backward from the shock of being slapped.

Oh, no, she didn't.

Just as I'm about to lunge at the ballerina so I can pull every last strand out of her neat bun, Dario's voice lashes through the air.

"What's going on here?"

"She stole my wedding ring," Vivian sobs before breaking down in a fit of tears.

Jesus, now's a good time to beam me up.

With my hand covering my stinging cheek, I stand frozen on the spot.

"I'm so sorry you had to walk in on such an unpleasant situation," Mrs. Stafford apologizes to Dario.

I feel him move closer to me and pinch my eyes shut.

God. God. God.

"Are you okay?" I hear him ask, and it makes my throat tighten with unshed tears because I'm still angry as hell, and now I'm embarrassed as well. I wish the ground would open beneath my feet.

This is not how I wanted him to find out.

Spinning around, I try to make a quick escape out of the office, which has Vivian screeching, "Stop her. She's trying to run away."

In the doorway, I bump into another ballerina and almost land on my ass as I fall against the doorjamb.

"Sorry," the ballerina says in a soft, sweet voice. "I just came to say I found the ring. It was in the restroom on the counter by the sinks."

I begin to slip past her, giving her a shaky smile, but I'm grabbed by my arm by Dario.

"Give me the ring, Izzy," he orders. When she places it in his palm, he says, "Go back to rehearsal."

I'm pulled into the office again, and feeling like I might burst out in tears like Vivian did, I clench my jaw tightly because I'm not some fragile ballerina.

Dario hands the ring to Vivian, then says, "You owe her an apology."

The fuck?

Before I can stop myself, my head snaps up, and I practically spit the words out. "I'm not apologizing for shit."

Dario's eyes latch onto my face, and as I watch recognition register on his face, followed shortly by absolute shock, my entire world tips on its axis.

I'm surprised when his tone is calm and steady when he says, "Vivian, apologize to Eden."

"I'm sorry," Vivian mutters.

His eyes narrow on my face, and then his features darken as if a storm is building, and I just know in my bones he's going to fire me.

It takes all my strength not to cry as a crack splinters down the middle of my heart. My voice is hoarse as I give him a pleading look. "I'm sorry. I was going to tell you tomorrow morning."

"We'll talk about that later," he snaps before his eyes flick to Mrs. Stafford. "Is this how you handle the staff?"

Mrs. Stafford instantly looks subdued as she says, "What was I to do? It was Vivian's word against the janitor's."

Dario lets go of my arm and moves slightly in front of me, his bicep brushing against my cap.

"Would you have dealt differently with the problem if you knew Eden's my girlfriend?"

I almost choke on a random drop of spit while Mrs. Stafford and Vivian gasp collectively.

"She's what?" Mrs. Stafford asks.

"Eden is my girlfriend," he repeats the words.

I watch as the women's attitudes shift, and where they were ready to tear me apart a moment ago, they give me apologetic looks.

Because of Dario.

"I'm so sorry, Miss Taylor. I wasn't aware of your relationship with Mr. La Rosa."

"Miss?" I let out a burst of incredulous laughter.

"I didn't mean to slap you," Vivian says.

Lifting my chin, I ask, "Can I go, Mrs. Stafford?"

"Of course. Let me know if you need anything," she says, her tone completely different from how she usually speaks to me.

Turning around, I walk out of the office. I go back to my cart, and determined to keep working until Dario tells me I'm fired, I grab the mop.

"We need to talk," Dario says behind me.

"I'm working," I mutter.

"Eden!"

I spin around. "I was going to tell you tomorrow."

"That you're a janitor?" he asks.

"Yes."

"Why didn't you tell me sooner?"

I give him an incredulous look. "Would you have still fucked me if you knew I worked for you?"

Slowly, he shakes his head. "Don't reduce our relationship to a simple fuck."

I suck in a shaky breath and try to regain control of my emotions, that are all over the place.

Dario takes hold of my hand and pulls me into the nearest studio. He shuts the door behind us, then turns to face me.

I lift my eyes to his face, and suddenly, it's getting harder and harder not to burst out in tears.

I do the only thing I can and say, "I'm sorry I didn't tell you sooner. I didn't want you to look at me and see a janitor. I wanted you to get to know me for who I am and not what I do, and...and." I swallow hard on the lump in my throat. "I was scared you'd fire me once you found out."

"I wouldn't have fired you," he murmurs softly.

"I know that now. That's why I was going to tell you tomorrow."

I rip off the stupid cap and wipe my palm over my hair.

The past hour hits me like a ton of bricks in the chest, and feeling smaller than a snail, I lower my head and stare at the scuff marks on my boots.

"It's unfair," I whisper.

"What?"

"They treated me like shit until they found out about our relationship. Mrs. Stafford has never been so nice to me."

I shake my head as my anger spikes again. A condescending chuckle escapes me as I lift my head to meet Dario's eyes.

"I was nothing in their eyes, then you come along, and with one sentence, their attitudes toward me change."

"I'm sorry, *Tesoro*. I'll deal with them."

What will everyone think of Dario? They'll laugh behind his back. The filthy rich guy and the poor as fuck janitor.

My heart hurts thinking Dario's reputation will suffer because of me.

Protecting him the only way I know how, I say, "It won't matter what you say to them or what you do. We come from different worlds, and everyone can see it. You live in a palace, and I can barely make rent. You eat at extravagant restaurants, and I..." I choke up and have to breathe through the chaotic emotions before I can continue, "It will never work between us."

"It can, and it will," Dario argues.

He steps closer to me, and placing his palm against the cheek Vivian slapped, he leans down to press a kiss to my mouth.

I close my eyes and take a deep breath of his scent.

I hope you find a woman worthy of being by your side and that she'll make you happier than I can.

When he lifts his head, I keep my eyes shut as the words spill from me, "It's too hard. I'm ending things now before one of us gets hurt."

"The fuck you are," he growls.

Opening my eyes, I look deep into his. It takes more strength than I have to ask, "You're not firing me, right?"

His eyebrows draw together, and he looks so angry I almost take a step backward but fight to stand my ground.

"I'm not firing you."

"Thank you."

I walk to the door and yank it open.

His tone is filled with determination as he snaps, "I'm not letting you end things between us."

When I step into the hallway, I hear him come after me, and a moment later, his fingers wrap around my arm, and I'm spun around to face him.

"Admit it. You want me as much as I want you. It doesn't fucking matter where we come from or who we are. All that matters is how we feel about each other."

I shake my head and lie through my teeth, "No. All I want is for things to go back to how they were before we met."

I can see my words are hurting Dario, and it makes it impossible for me to hold the tears in.

As they roll over my cheeks, I whisper, "You're an amazing man, Dario. I'll always treasure our time together."

"Stop!" he snaps, then he yanks me against his chest.

Before I can push away from him, his arms lock around me, keeping me imprisoned in his hold.

His irises turn black, and with a dangerous expression tightening his features, he says, "You are mine. I will never let you go."

I try to push against his chest, which only makes him tighten his hold on me. When it borders on painful, I whisper, "You're hurting me."

Instantly, Dario lets go of me, and as worry blends with the anger on his face, I say, "I'm okay. You just held me too tight."

He shoves his hand through his hair. "I'm sorry, *Tesoro*."

I give him a pleading look. "I need to get back to work."

He nods, then says, "When I'm done with the rehearsals, I'll come to find you so we can talk without people accidentally hearing us."

Nodding, I walk back toward my cart, and grabbing the mop, I fight the urge to glance over my shoulder.

All I want to do is run into Dario's arms, but instead, I focus on cleaning the floor.

Chapter 19

Dario

I can't focus on the rehearsal, and halfway through, I hold a hand in the air and say, "Everyone go home. Come in an hour earlier tomorrow."

Mrs. Stafford gets up from where she's sitting and heads in my direction.

When she stops near me, I mutter, "Go home. I'll talk to you tomorrow."

"I just want to apologize again. I should've handled the situation better. It won't happen again."

I take my phone out to show her she's dismissed and press dial on Eden's number.

It rings longer than usual before Eden answers, "Hi."

"Come to the auditorium."

"Okay."

While I wait, I think about how many times I saw Eden cleaning, and not once did I recognize her. Upset with myself, I stare at the empty stage.

Now, it makes sense how she managed to evade me after dancing.

When she comes into the auditorium via the side door, I stand up and move out of the aisle. Taking the steps down, I meet her in front of the stage.

I reach for the cap and take it off her head. Wrapping my fingers around the back of her neck, I lean down and press a tender kiss to her mouth.

When I pull back, my lock eyes with hers. "None of the we-come-from-different-worlds-shit matters to me. I want you exactly as you are, Eden."

The fight has left her eyes, and when a tear sneaks down her cheek, I brush it away with my thumb.

"I just don't want to embarrass you," she admits.

"You can never do that."

"People will talk," she whispers.

"I don't care what other people think. I only care about us," I assure her.

She stares at me for a moment before wrapping her arms around my waist and burying her face against my chest.

"I'm sorry about tonight," she says, her voice hoarse with tears. "I didn't want you to find out like this."

"It's okay. I understand why you were hesitant to tell me."

It's the same reason I haven't told her about the Cosa Nostra. I'd be a hypocrite if I held it against her.

I can only hope she'll show me the same understanding when I tell her I'm a mafia boss.

I rub my hand up and down her back a few times before I take hold of her jaw and nudge her face up so she'll look at me.

"I don't want to hear anything about us ending things again. Okay?"

"Okay."

I give her a kiss, then ask, "Will you dance for me?"

A smile tugs at her mouth as she nods. "Let me just change clothes."

"Come with me." I take her hand, and leading her backstage to where various outfits for the show are standing in rows, I look through them until I find the perfect one for Eden.

"Put this on."

Her eyes flit between my face and the dress before she takes hold of it.

"I'll wait in the studio for you."

Walking away, I suck in a relieved breath of air.

Thank fuck she didn't keep fighting me on the 'difference' thing. I get that it will take time for her to adjust to my lifestyle, and I'll be as patient as she needs me to be.

Reaching the studio, I shrug my suit jacket off and drop it on one of the chairs before I take a seat. I unbutton the cuffs of my long-sleeve shirt, and roll them up to my elbows while I wait for Eden to come.

Tomorrow, I'll give Mrs. Stafford a final warning and deal with Vivian. There's no way she's dancing for my company after she slapped my woman.

When Eden walks into the studio, wearing a white body suit that's studded with diamante, my lips curve up. Chiffon falls around her like a cape, gliding around her with every step she takes.

She connects her phone to the speakers, and just like the last time she danced for me, she moves closer to me until she rests her palm against my jaw.

Never Let Me Go by *Florence & The Machines* begins to fill the air. I turn my face and press a kiss to her palm, and a second later, she's twirling away from me.

As I watch my woman dance for me, the stress caused by the shitshow a couple of hours ago rolls off my shoulders. My muscles relax, and I get lost in the sparkle of the diamante and the passion she exudes as her body moves across the floor.

As the song comes to an end, I get up and walk to where her phone is lying. I disconnect her device, before connecting my own. Searching for the right song, I press play before I walk to where Eden is standing.

I wrap my arm around her as *You're Still You* by *Josh Groban* begins to play. Slowly, I guide her over the floor, hoping she's listening to the words.

Her eyes begin to shimmer with unshed tears, and she wraps her arms around my neck, holding me as tight as she can. I keep moving to the beat of the music as I savor the feel of her body against mine.

When the song reaches its climax, I lower my head and kiss her with every ounce of emotion she stirs in my heart.

This woman danced her way right into my heart.

Right now, it feels like I've found the one who was always meant for me.

My other half.

At some point we stop dancing, just enjoying the kiss.

When I finally lift my head, a soft smile curves her swollen lips.

"Okay."

I give her a questioning look. "Okay?"

"You never asked, but okay, I'll be your girlfriend."

Laughter bursts from me, and I squash her against my chest.

I press a kiss to the top of her head, then say, "As your boss, I'm giving you the rest of the night off."

She pulls back and shakes her head. "No. Let me do my job. It's important to me."

"Then I'll help so I can spend more time with you."

She starts to chuckle. "You're going to help me clean?"

"Yes."

"Okay." She pulls out of my arms and walks to the door. "I'm just going to change."

I follow her to the dressing rooms at the back of the stage and watch as she changes back into her clothes.

After she puts on the apron, she picks up the cap and plops it down on top of my head while saying, "Come on. We have a lot to do."

I follow her to where she left her cart and mutter, "Put me to work."

"Oh, you're going to regret saying that," she teases. She pushes the cart to the auditorium, then orders, "You can vacuum while I polish the stage."

"Okay."

Eden shows me how the vacuum cleaner works, and when she's happy with how I do it, she heads up to the stage.

We keep stealing glances at each other, and when we're finally done, I get rewarded with a kiss.

Chapter 20

Eden

When Tyrone opens his front door, I ask, "Want to come dress shopping with me?"

He lets out a sigh, then mutters, "Let me grab my coat."

I grin at him, and when he's done locking the door behind him, I hook my arm through his. "I need a fancy dress for a ballet show. I'm going as Dario's date."

Tyrone's eyes widen on me as we take the stairs down to the exit.

"Does that mean he knows you work for him?"

I nod. "Last night, shit went down at the ballet company. One of the ballerinas accused me of stealing her wedding ring."

Instantly angry, Tyrone snaps, "The bitch."

"Yeah. She slapped me just as Dario came into the office." I shake my head. "He was so angry I thought for sure I was done for."

"Why was he angry at you?!" he exclaims.

"No, not at me. He was angry at Mrs. Stafford and Vivian – she's the one who slapped me."

When we step out onto the sidewalk, we both notice Junior at the same time where he's standing across the road.

"What are you doing here?" Tyrone shouts.

"Just keeping the street clean," Junior replies.

"So weird," I mutter as we head in the direction of the bus stop.

"Yeah," he whispers. "It feels like they're gearing up for shit to go down."

Tyrone wraps his arm around my shoulder, and we walk a little faster.

"So, what happened after Dario walked in on the bitch slapping you?"

I continue telling Tyrone how Dario stood up for me and assured me he doesn't care about the differences between us.

"Sounds like he's madly in love with you," he chuckles. "Look at my girl landing herself a big fish."

"Dario's not a big fish," I mutter. A grin spreads over my face. "I swear he's perfect. Sometimes, I wish he'd do something wrong so I won't feel so imperfect next to him."

"You're good people, Eden. The man is lucky to have you."

"Yeah?"

"Yeah," he murmurs, giving me a loving smile.

We don't have to wait long at the bus stop, and soon, we're heading in the direction of the thrift store.

"Feels like we're going dress shopping for your prom," Tyrone mutters.

I let out a chuckle. "Remember the ugly purple one I wore? I looked like candyfloss."

"You looked pretty," he argues.

"I always look pretty to you."

"That's because you're my girl."

I lean my head on his shoulder, feeling so happy nothing can ruin my mood.

When the bus stops, we step off and walk the short distance to our destination.

Entering the thrift store, I say, "Hi, Lisa. I'm looking for your prettiest but cheapest dress."

"Fuck that," Tyrone argues. "I'm paying. Show her your best dresses."

"No, Tyrone," I whisper.

He pats my back before nudging me toward Lisa. "Let me do this for my daughter."

My heart squeezes, and I have to blink like crazy as love for the man fills my chest.

Lisa digs through all the dresses, and we find quite a few pretty ones.

"You might want to take a seat," I laugh at Tyrone before I disappear behind the curtain of the dressing room.

"Get me a chair," I hear him tell Lisa.

I put on a black, tight-fitting one, but I already don't like the way the fabric falls stiff over my hips. I try to smooth it out with my hands as I pull the curtain back.

Tyrone takes a moment to look, then mutters, "Too little fabric. It's winter."

"I'll wear a coat," I argue as I pull the curtain shut again.

Dress after dress is a no from Tyrone, and I'm busy working up a sweat.

The last one is a Morticia-Adams-type mermaid gown with beads down the front. At first glance, I didn't think I'd like it, but the moment I have it on, I stare at myself in the mirror with my lips parted.

Slowly, a smile spreads over my face, and it only gets bigger when I pull the curtain back.

Again, Tyrone takes his time to look at the dress, then his eyes lock on my face, and he nods. "That's the one."

"Right? It makes me look like a queen."

"Definitely. Get changed so we can pay. I want a hot dog from the stand on the corner."

"Only if the hot dog is my treat."

Tyrone mutters something under his breath while I close the curtain and quickly change back into my jeans and sweater. I shrug on my coat, and with the dress hanging over my arm, I walk to the counter.

A couple of minutes later, we leave the store, and as we stop to get two hot dogs, one of Frankie's men drives slowly past us.

An uneasy feeling skitters down my spine.

Tyrone's right. It feels as if there's a storm brewing in the air.

After Tyrone's eaten half his hot dog, he says, "You know what would be nice?"

"What?"

"That cheesecake you got me a couple of weeks ago."

"It was from the Starbucks near work. Want me to get you one tomorrow?"

"Yeah. You'd make your old man happy."

We enjoy our food while we wait for a bus. When it comes, we have to stand because all the seats are taken.

During the ride, I glance down at the bag in my hand, hoping Dario will like the dress.

I just need to touch up my black heels with a marker, and I'll be good to go. I'm going to style my hair in soft curls. The smoky look around my eyes with red lipstick will be a good fit with the dress.

Excitement bubbles in my chest, and I can't wait for tomorrow.

Dario

When Eden opens her front door, my lips part as I'm struck in the heart by how beautiful she looks.

Christ, I'm lucky.

I stand rooted to the spot, taking in every inch of her. The dress fits her like a glove, accentuating her curves.

Finally I manage to murmur, "You look breathtaking, *Tesoro*."

The happiest smile I've ever seen brightens up her face. "Yeah?"

I nod as I take a step forward, and wrapping my arm around her waist, I tug her against my body.

"I'm at a loss for words," I admit before I press a soft kiss to the corner of her mouth, being careful not to smudge her lipstick.

The eyeshadow she's wearing makes the gray in her eyes look more prominent.

"Have I mentioned you have beautiful eyes?" I ask.

She shakes her head as she rubs her palms up and down my biceps.

"They're stunning, *Tesoro*."

"Thanks." She pulls back and looks at the tuxedo I'm wearing. "You look way too handsome, Mr. La Rosa."

"Thank you." I nod toward the stairs. "Let's go."

Taking Eden's hand, I link our fingers, and when we leave the building, I notice one of Frankie's men.

When he gives us a chin lift, Eden mutters, "Don't mind him. He claims he's keeping the street clean. I think something's about to go down. That's why they're all over the neighborhood."

"Yeah?" I murmur as I glance around us.

She squeezes my hand. "Don't worry. I'll protect you."

I let out a burst of laughter, and finding her fucking adorable, I wrap her in a tight hug before I open the R8's passenger door.

When the engine roars to life, Frankie's man grins with approval. To make the man's day, I floor the gas, and we shoot down the street.

Eden's laughter fills the car, her nails digging into my thigh.

I slow down until I'm no longer breaking the speed limit and place my hand on top of hers.

This feels right.

The only thing that would make things perfect is if Eden moved in with me.

"Are you excited for tonight?" she asks.

"Yes. Besides everyone working hard to make tonight possible, I can't wait to introduce you to all of my friends."

AKA the other heads of the Cosa Nostra.

She smooths her free hand over her dress. "I'm glad I look my best. I hope they like me."

"They'll love you."

Eden might not know it yet, but as my girlfriend, she's one of the most protected women in New York.

I bring the R8 to a stop in front of the ballet company, where a red carpet has been rolled up.

The two men who've been hired as valets open our doors, and when we climb out of the vehicle, cameras start flashing.

Eden dips her head low as she hurries to my side. I wrap my arm around her lower back and hold her close as we walk from reporter to reporter.

"Is it true the show is sold out?" one asks as flashes blind us.

"Yes," I answer, a professional smile on my face.

"Who's the woman by your side," another reporter shouts over the crowd.

Pride fills my chest as I say, "My girlfriend, Eden Taylor."

When a reporter calls out, "Is the ballet company a front for money laundering?" I usher Eden into the building before the fucker can give away that I'm Cosa Nostra.

"Wow. That wasn't intense at all," she murmurs by my side while a nervous expression tightens her features.

"Luckily, it doesn't happen often," I say as I lead her to the waiting area outside the auditorium.

Seeing Renzo, Skylar, Angelo, and Vittoria, I walk toward them.

It takes a moment to introduce Eden to my friends and their better halves, then I say, "Thanks for coming."

Angelo nods. "Damiano said he might be a couple of minutes late."

"Evening, everyone," Franco says behind us.

I turn around and shake his hand, then quickly introduce him and Samantha to Eden, who's glued to my side, her eyes darting between my friends.

Meeting them all at once can be a bit intimidating.

A server offers us a flute of champagne, which Samantha and Vittoria decline because they're both pregnant.

"I love your dress," Skylar tells Eden.

"Thank you," my woman answers, a smile tugging at her red lips. "You all look beautiful too."

"If I didn't force Skylar to change, she would've come in her chef's uniform," Renzo mutters.

"Oh, right. We were at your restaurant a while back," Eden mentions. "The food was great."

"I'm glad you enjoyed it."

Seeing how my friends are trying to make Eden feel comfortable makes me love them so much more.

People part like the sea, then I see the reason why. Damiano walks toward us with a thunderous expression darkening his face.

When he reaches us, I mutter, "Can you please smile? You're scaring my guests."

He scowls at me, then says, "We're meeting at my place after the show. There's shit we have to discuss."

I widen my eyes at him before nodding at Eden. "Work can wait. This is my girlfriend, Eden Taylor."

Damiano just nods in her direction, not sparing her a glance.

Angelo throws his arm around Damiano's shoulder and steers him toward the area where a bar has been set up.

Leaning down, I murmur near Eden's ear, "Don't mind him. He's always like a bear with a sore tooth."

"Okay."

"Yeah," Samantha agrees. "He's all growl but no bite."

Unless you piss him off.

For the next thirty minutes, I greet some of the important guests with Eden on my arm, and by the time we head into the auditorium to take our seats, she lets out a breath of relief.

"Did I do okay?" she asks as I gesture for her to sit.

"Yes. You were perfect," I compliment her, and unbuttoning my jacket, I take the seat beside her.

On my other side, Renzo fakes a yawn. "Wake me up when the show's over."

I elbow him in the side. "Fall asleep, and I'll punch you."

The lights dim, and a spotlight focuses on the stage.

As the show starts, I take hold of Eden's hand and places it on my thigh. Brushing my thumb over her soft skin, I watch as the past year's hard work pays off.

Chapter 21

Eden

During an intense scene where the ballerinas are twirling and flying through the air, my phone starts to ring.

"Shit," I whisper. Grabbing my handbag, I dig the device out so I can silence it, but when I see Tyrone's name on the screen, I answer and say, "Give me a minute."

I shoot Dario an apologetic look before I get up and quickly leave the auditorium.

The music is still loud as I walk down a hallway, and holding the phone to my ear, I say, "What's up?"

"Yo- need t-."

"Hold on, the reception is bad," I mutter, hoping he can hear me.

The call is disconnected, and once I reach the lobby and make sure all the reporters are gone, I dial Tyrone's number while stepping out on the sidewalk.

"Hey, can you hear me?" his voice comes clearer over the line.

"Yeah. Why are you calling?"

Jesus, it's cold. I should've brought my coat.

"Shit went down. Men came looking for you and Mandy, and when Junior confronted them, the fuckers shot him."

"What?" I gasp as shock vibrates through me.

"Don't come home tonight. Go to Dario's place. Frankie said he'd take care of shit here."

"Is Junior okay?" I ask. I might not like the gangster, but hearing he got shot because of Mandy sucks.

"They rushed him to the hospital. I don't know how he's doing," Tyrone says, his voice tense. "You need to be careful. I'm going to check Mandy's usual hangouts."

"No!" I exclaim. "Stay away from her. I don't–"

My words are cut off when a van comes to a screeching stop in the street. When men pour out of the vehicle, I spin around and rush back into the lobby.

"They're here."

"Run, Eden!" Tyrone's worried voice comes over the line.

"What's wrong?" Quincy asks.

"Run. Run. Run," I shout at the guard.

I'm grabbed from behind, and my phone flies out of my hand.

Oh shit!

When Quincy reaches for his gun, a shot is fired near my ear, instantly robbing me of my hearing.

All I hear is a sharp buzzing sound as I watch Quincy drop to the floor. My heart instantly thunders in my chest, and a terrifying sensation spreads over my skin.

"No!" I scream as I'm lifted off my feet and dragged out of the lobby.

I begin to thrash, trying to hit and kick my way out of the predicament I find myself in.

I'm hauled to the van and roughly tossed inside the vehicle. Before I can catch my bearings, more hands grab at me, restraining my wrists with cable ties.

"Stop. Stop," I gasp, just needing a second to gather myself so I can think clearer.

The van speeds away with screeching tires, and I struggle to keep my balance as we swerve around a corner.

One of the men grabs me by the back of my hair, pulling strands out, then he forces me to look at another man who's staring at me.

"Where's your bitch of a mother?"

"I don't know, and she's not my mother," I spit out.

"She owes me thirty thousand dollars."

I try to lift my chin to appear braver than I feel. "Not my problem."

The corner of his mouth lifts slightly before he backhands me across the cheek. I feel my lip split as pain explodes behind my right eye.

"If Mandy's not gonna settle her debt, you will," he barks in my direction.

My tongue darts out, tasting the blood on my lip, then I say, "I don't have any money."

The man stares at me for a few unnerving seconds before he lets out a dark chuckle, "If you can't pay in cash, you'll just have to work off the debt."

Work off the debt?

No.

I start to shake my head, my heart clenching with fear as I realize what kind of work I'll be doing.

Prostitution.

Either that, or I'll be forced to be a drug mule.

Both options suck ass.

"Let me go, and I'll find a way to get the money," I try to bargain with the drug dealer.

He tilts his head while his eyes rove over the dress I'm wearing, then he mutters, "How do you plan to make thirty thousand in twenty-four hours?"

Jesus. That's impossible.

"I need more time." *Like a year or so.*

He leans back in his seat and crosses his legs. "You see, that's my problem. I don't have any time. My boss wants his thirty thousand now."

Fuck you, Mandy. I swear if I ever see you again, I'm going to kill you.

"I don't see why I have to pay Mandy's debt. She's not my mother," I say, even though I know it won't matter to these people.

He shrugs, not replying to what I just said. Taking a pack of smokes out, he lights one, giving me the impression he's done talking.

I glance at the five men while wiggling my hands, but when the plastic digs into my skin, I stop. I look out the windows as we cross a bridge and wonder where they're taking me.

I swallow to ease the dryness in my throat, then ask, "Where are we going?"

The man next to me hisses, "Shut up."

"I just want–"

I'm slapped upside the head, the force of the blow stunning my mind, but it doesn't stop me from stomping on the asshole's boot with my five-inch heel.

"Give her something to relax," the main guy mutters while flicking ash on the floor.

My eyes widen, and I shake my head wildly. "I'll keep quiet."

One of the assholes pulls an injection from his pocket, and when he takes the cap off, I'm up off the seat and staggering around in the small space in an attempt to get away from him.

I'm shoved off my feet, and when I hit the floor, I'm pushed onto my stomach. The needle breaking through the skin on the inside of my forearm rips a cry from me.

I've seen how drugs have destroyed lives.

How it eats Mandy alive.

As a weird sensation starts to dull my mind, I gasp against the floor.

With every passing second, my body feels more and more sluggish, and my reality warps. It feels as if I'm stuck in a world where things spin too fast and super slow at the same time.

I'm left on the floor for the duration of the ride, lights and shadows blurring before my eyes.

Dario

When it feels like Eden's been gone a long while, I get up and head out of the auditorium to see if she's okay.

I don't find her right outside the doors, and when I walk toward the lobby, I hear a phone ringing briefly before stopping.

As I reach the front desk, my eyes land on Quincy, unconscious next to his desk, and the phone starts ringing again.

"Fuck," I gasp, and ignoring the device, I hurry to the security guard.

Seeing blood pooling beneath the side he's lying on, shock vibrates through me. I dig my cell phone out and call 911, telling them to get an ambulance to the ballet company.

Glancing around to make sure there's no immediate danger I have to deal with, I push Quincy onto his back, which has him groaning something I can't make out.

"It's okay. An ambulance is coming," I say, hoping he can hear me. "What happened?"

"E…den," he gasps.

My body stills as an intensely destructive emotion bleeds through my chest.

"What about Eden?"

The fucking phone keeps ringing, and when Quincy glances at it, I get up and stalk to the device vibrating on the tiled floor.

Seeing Tyrone's name on the screen, I glance around the lobby for Eden while I answer, "It's Dario."

"Fuck. The fucking motherfuckers took her. Call the cops. They fucking grabbed her while I was on the phone with her," he shouts, his anger and worry out of control.

Ice floods my veins, and everything becomes eerily still in me. My tone sounds emotionless as I ask, "Who?"

"The dealers who are looking for that piece-of-shit mother of hers. They came by the apartment and shot another thug before taking off again. I called Eden to tell her not to come home."

"I'll find her," I assure him.

"I'm calling the cops," he tells me.

"They won't find her in time," I snap, and not giving a flying shit, I say, "The Cosa Nostra will handle this."

"The fuck you just say?" he gasps.

"My people and I will deal with this problem."

"The mafia. You're mafia?" he asks, his tone filled with disbelief.

"Yes. Don't do anything, Tyrone. I'll find Eden," I order before I end the call and tuck her phone into my pocket.

When an ambulance stops in front of the building, I wait until they're tending to Quincy before I leave the lobby.

Walking to my car, I send a text to the group chat.

Dario: Miguel's men grabbed Eden. I'm going after them.

As I slide behind the steering wheel, one text after another makes my phone vibrate like crazy.

Renzo: On my way.

Franco: Wait for us.

Angelo: I'll get my men ready.

Damiano: We'll meet at your place and take things from there.

I ignore the speed limits as I race home and don't even bother parking the R8 in the designated spot. Darting out of the vehicle, I rush to the elevator and slam the button repeatedly.

My patience wears thinner and thinner as I ride up to my floor, and when the doors open, I run into my apartment.

"What's wrong?" Esmerelda calls out as I dodge Bella and take the stairs two at a time to get to my office, where my system is set up.

I switch everything on, and while the monitors flicker to life, I shrug off my jacket and drop it on the floor. Taking a seat, my fingers begin to fly over the keyboard, and information starts appearing on the monitors.

I pull up CCTV camera feeds around the ballet company, and scanning a photo of Eden into the system, I'm able to get footage from outside the Starbucks. It's grainy and dark, but I'm able to make out as men drag Eden out of the building before shoving her into a van.

Knowing they can change the number plate of the van at any given moment, I quickly punch the numbers into my system and start to track the van from CCTV camera to camera.

Suddenly, Renzo and Franko rush into my office, and Renzo asks, "What do you have?"

"I'm tracking a van that's heading toward Brooklyn," I mutter, my fingers not stopping for a second.

"Elio and my men are on their way," Renzo says.

"Marcello and Milo are also coming with some of mine. I'm leaving a group to watch our women while we deal with this problem," Franco says.

Connecting the system to my tablet so I can track them while on the go, I get up and rush to the cabinet where I keep my weapons. Unlocking the door, I swing it open and grab two Heckler & Kochs with extra magazines.

"Dario," Renzo says to get my attention, but I'm too busy grabbing a K-Bar knife and strapping it to my thigh.

"Dario!" Franco snaps while grabbing my shoulder.

Swinging around, I shove him out of my way and race out of the office.

"Christ," Renzo curses, and I hear them come after me. "Let's wait until everyone's here."

"No," I mutter, and as I take the stairs down, it's to see half an army already standing in my living room and foyer.

Ignoring everyone, I head to the elevator, but Damiano steps into my path, and shakes his head, an expression I seldom see on his face darkening his features.

"Stop," he orders, his tone filled with dominance.

Having the *capo dei capi* issue an order, years of respect forces me to a halt in front of him.

He places his hand on my shoulder and locks eyes with mine. "We're doing this as a family."

When he squeezes my shoulder before pulling away, I'm actually a little stunned because Damiano doesn't show kindness easily.

"Franco and Renzo will travel together," he says. "Dario and Angelo's with me. When we catch up to Miguel's men, I only need one alive enough to be questioned, the rest I want dead."

I check my tablet and say, "It doesn't look like they're stopping in Brooklyn."

Damiano glances at Carlo, who's his underboss. "Make sure my private jet is fueled and ready to go, in case they try to take a flight out of here. Also, prepare a helicopter and boat. I want all escape routes covered." He turns around and walks to the elevator while muttering, "We're taking the war to them. Wherever the fuck they go."

As I step into the elevator with the other heads and a few of our men, Damiano tells Carlo, "Find out where Miguel's family is and send men to get them."

My eyes are glued to the screen of my tablet, and I watch as notification after notification pops up, showing they're taking Eden farther and farther away from me.

We're coming, Tesoro.

Chapter 22

Eden

I feel completely disorientated and helpless as I'm lugged over a shoulder and carried somewhere.

Sounds come and go, not really registering.

I lose touch with reality, and when I come to enough to make sense of my surroundings, I hear a motor droning and water splashing.

My body's shivering uncontrollably from the ice-cold air blowing over me, and I manage to let out a groan.

"How was the high, babe?" A man asks.

High?

Babe?

Where am I?

I have to fight to pry my eyes open, but my vision keeps going in and out of focus.

Someone slaps my cheek lightly, then a man laughs, "She's still out of it."

I realize I'm in a boat as it starts to slow down, and a minute or so later, I'm hauled over a shoulder again.

I manage to make out a bigger boat, and some control over my body begins to return. Bile churns in the pit of my stomach, and for a moment, it feels like I'm going to puke.

I'm tossed down on a hard surface, and the back of my head takes a knock, drawing another groan from me.

I have…to get…up.

My head rolls to the side, and I watch as men sit down on leather seats before the bigger boat starts to move.

Where are they taking me?

Finally whatever they gave wears off enough that I'm able to lift my head. Feeling sluggish, I pull myself up into a sitting position, bracing my back against the side of the boat.

"I thought you said she's still out of it," one of the men mutters.

"Should I shoot her up again?"

"Nah, the shit's too expensive to waste on her."

"Where…am I?" I ask, my voice slurred.

"The wide-open sea, babe."

As my mind clears up more, I remember the drug dealers grabbing me and saying I have to pay off Mandy's debt.

Oh, God.

The thought has my senses returning full force, and I glance around as I climb to my feet.

There are only three men on the boat with me. For an insane moment, I contemplate jumping overboard, but with my wrists tied, I'll drown.

"Want to skinny dip?" one of the assholes ask before he bursts out laughing.

"No, thanks. It's a bit too cold for that shit," I mutter, feeling calmer than I should.

Losing my cool will only get me killed.

Jesus, I'm thirsty.

"Is there anything to drink?" I ask as I move to an open seat and sit down.

"No food and drinks on this cruise, babe," one of them answers me with a smirk.

The wind is fucking cold, and it feels as if I'm turning blue, which has me snapping, "Is there a blanket or something I can use to keep warm?"

The one who talked to me the most nods his head at me. "She's starting to annoy me. Shoot her up."

"No!" I cry as an injection is dug out of a pocket. "I'll shut up."

One of the assholes gives me a evil-as-fuck grin before saying, "Too late."

When I dart up, I'm knocked off my feet, and once again, I find myself face down as a needle is stuck into my arm.

Shit.

No.

"Stop."

"I'll shut...up."

"D..on't."

The world warps, and suddenly, I don't feel so cold anymore.

Dario

We're an hour behind the fuckers, which has given them one hell of a head start.

The van stopped near a marina and is now heading back in our direction. Which could mean they either dropped Eden off or worse.

"Give or take twenty minutes until we'll cross paths with them," I mutter.

Carlo is behind the steering wheel, Damiano's in the passenger seat, and I'm in the back with Angelo.

Damiano glances over his shoulder and mutters, "You know how this goes, Dario. If Eden's mother owes them money, they've probably handed her over to another crew who'll make her work to pay off the debt."

The thought had already crossed my mind, but I instantly shunned it. Having Damiano say it out loud makes a growl build in my chest.

My tone is filled with rage as I say, "Over my dead body, am I letting them use my woman as a prostitute."

"It won't come to that," Angelo murmurs, his tone much calmer than I feel. "We'll get to her in time."

My eyes remain glued to the road ahead, and it takes way too fucking long before we see the van.

"Hold on," Carlo mutters.

The next second he slams on the breaks as he makes a sharp turn.

All the SUVs behind us form a barricade in case the van gets past us.

I shove the door open, and as I climb out, I pull my two guns from behind my back, where they are tucked into my waistband. I raise my arms and train the barrels on the windscreen.

"Where the fuck is Eden?" I shout.

The drug dealers look stunned for a couple of seconds, then they pile out of the van.

I open fire, and I'm backed up by more shots being fired by my friends.

As one of the fuckers drops from a gunshot to the leg, I move in on him and step on his hand so he'll let go of his gun.

The gunfire ends as abruptly as it started, and Carlo comes to haul the remaining fucker, who's still alive, to his feet. He struggles to stand as Damiano nods for me to do my thing.

"What did you do with Eden?"

The drug dealer gives me a look filled with disrespect, which has me swinging my fist at his face.

"What did you do with my woman?" I ask again.

He spits blood out of his mouth, then mutters, "The bitch is gone."

His words shudder through me.

"Gone as in dead, or on her way to work as a prostitute?" Damiano asks, his tone dark and impatient.

The drug dealer grins, his teeth covered in blood. "Does it matter?"

Losing his patience, Damiano shoots the man in his foot, making him collapse to the gravel.

"Traffic is starting to pile up on either side of us," Angelo says. "We need to go."

"Tell us where she is, and we'll let you live," Franco mutters.

"She was transferred to a boat," the dealer fesses up. "I don't know what happens to the girls after we hand them over."

Damiano nods with his head. "Run."

The fucker stumbles to his feet and starts hopping toward a nearby field, his useless leg being dragged behind him.

Raising my arm, I take aim, and with a single shot to his head, I drop his ass on the side of the road.

"No one lives," I mutter as I turn around and walk back to the SUV.

Climbing in, I grab my tablet and open a different app where I begin hacking into law enforcement programs that monitor vessels electronically.

I'm aware of everyone getting back into the SUV and that we're moving again, but I don't glance up as I look for a way to find out where Eden could be.

"We're going to the airfield," Damiano instructs Carlo. "We need to get airborne."

Chapter 23

Eden

Opening my eyes, I find myself upside down as I'm lugged over a shoulder again.

The world sways, and I manage to see a short hallway with steps leading up to what I assume is a deck.

I'm still on a boat?

I hear a door open, and a second later, I'm tossed on the floor like a sack of potatoes. A groan escapes me, and when my eyes focus on the man who threw me down, I don't recognize him. He's dressed in a suit instead of regular clothes like the others were.

"Remove the dress and shoes," he mutters before walking out of the room and shutting the door behind him.

Huh?

I'm grabbed by my arms and hauled to my feet, and when I hear the zipper of my dress go down, the lingering effects of the drugs they gave me vanish at the speed of light.

"The hell," I snap, but it sounds more surprised than angry.

I begin to twist and turn my body while slapping at the hands reaching for me. There's a hard blow to the side of my head that makes me fall on my hip.

I push through the pain, and when I lift my head, I see four women standing in a row by a wall. One stares at me with a blank look, while the other three have silent tears rolling down their cheeks.

I'm hauled back to my feet, and as my head whips around, I see two men who again try to remove my dress.

"Don't fucking touch me," I shout.

It takes another precious second for it to sink in that I'm in a fuck-ton of trouble.

A panicked chuckle escapes me, then I swing around and dart for the door.

One of the men grabs me by the hair and slams me face-first into the door I was hoping to escape through, then I'm yanked backward. The sound of tearing fabric hits my ears as the dress is forcefully ripped from my body.

Jesus.

God.

I suck in trembling breaths, my eyes flitting wildly from the girls to the men to the rest of the empty room.

There are two small oval-shaped windows, and through them, I can see dark, choppy waters.

Standing in my black bra and panties, the survival instinct that's kept me alive since birth kicks in. I grab the shoe off my right foot, and with a cry, I lunge at the closest man, burying the five-inch heel in his eye socket.

When it registers what I've just done, I watch with horrified shock as he falls to the floor. I gag at the gross sight covering my mouth with my hand.

I'm untied?

When did they untie me?

My eyes land on the torn dress that Tyrone bought for me.

He worked hard for that money.

He was so proud of me when he saw how beautiful I looked in it.

Again, I look at the man who looks way too dead for my liking.

I killed someone.

With a shoe.

Shit, now I'm short a shoe.

I'm tackled off my feet, and as I fall, my eyes latch onto the man with my heel buried in his eye.

He's really dead. Like dead dead.

I hit the floor with a painful thud, and it rips me out of the shock I was caught in. My arms fly up, and with angry grunts and cries, I hit every part of the other man I can reach.

I bring my knee up and slam it into his balls, which has him falling to the side with a funny squeak escaping him.

"Jesus," I mutter as I climb to my feet, and taking off my other shoe, I hold it ready in my hands. "Come on. I'll fucking kill you, you motherfucking piece of shit. I loved that dress!"

I lunge at him and start hitting him with the heel of my shoe until he manages to grab his gun.

When he aims it at me, I jump off him and shriek, "Oh shit."

A stupid nervous chuckle escapes me before I suck in a ragged breath.

Shitshitshitshitshit.

He keeps the gun pointed at me as he climbs to his feet, then hisses, "*La perra*," right before he slams the weapon against the side of my head, knocking me unconscious.

Dario

We had to split up. Renzo and Franco stayed behind to make sure their women and Vittoria got home safely after the ballet show.

Damiano, Angelo, and I are in a helicopter that Carlo is flying. We're searching the fucking ocean for any boat that looks suspicious, which is like looking for a needle in a haystack. Especially at night.

"This is taking too long," Damiano mutters.

"No fucking shit," I growl as I check the dark web for any information that can help me find Eden.

"I'm picking up activity in the air," Carlo suddenly says. "Three helicopters."

"And?" Damiano barks.

"They're all flying in the same direction," Carlo answers.

"Not odd at all," Angelo mentions.

"Follow them," I order. "It's a shot in the dark, but it's better than flying around until we run out of fuel."

I keep looking for any leads we can use, and as time crawls by, my worry for Eden grows.

It's hard not to think of what the fuckers could be doing to her. Being a criminal myself, I know how ugly the world really is.

A thought pops into my mind, and I search for private parties with a hefty price tag. There are hundreds, and I add words related to water, seeing as Eden has been taken by boat.

What I find chills me to my bone.

$50000. Fishing trip. N/V. Use/Dispose.

"Fuck," I whisper as my heart beat faster.

"What?"

"There's a private party where women can be used or killed. Whoever scores a ticket can do whatever they want," I translate the information I found.

"Eden's not at that party," Angelo says. "It's all too convenient."

"It's sold as a fishing trip," I snap. "I'll bet everything I have those helicopters are flying to the yacht where this party is being held, and if there's a chance that Eden could be there, I'm going."

Damiano nods his approval. "It's the only lead we have."

"Let's hope they're expecting a fourth helicopter," Carlo mutters.

Chapter 24

Dario

Carlo has to circle the boat as the helicopters take turns to land and drop off their passengers.

We wait until last before Carlo sets us down on the supersized yacht. Angelo shoves the door open and gets out first, followed by me, then Damiano.

A man dressed in a tuxedo frowns at us. "We weren't expecting a fourth party."

An armed guard gives us a wary look, his fingers twitching around his weapon.

"We invited ourselves," I mutter, impatient to search the yacht so I can find Eden.

Another man, who's escorted by two guards, comes up the stairs, and his eyes lock instantly on Damiano. "What's the Cosa Nostra doing here? This isn't your territory."

I glance at Damiano. "You know him?"

"Kristian," my boss murmurs. "Sex trafficker. Let me handle this." Damiano takes a step forward and lets out a sigh. "I'm here for a specific girl."

"We don't have anyone who belongs to the Cosa Nostra," the man replies calmly, as if he isn't worried we'll kill him.

"Show us the girls, and we'll be on our way," Damiano mutters.

"Only you. The rest wait right here," the man agrees.

Not happy, I cross my arms over my chest and watch as Damiano and Carlo follow the man.

When a guard shakes his head at Carlo, Damiano says, "Where I go, he goes."

"Let him come," the man snaps, clearly starting to lose his patience with the situation.

We don't wait long before Damiano and Carlo come back. My boss shakes his head, then orders, "Let's go. We're wasting our time here."

For a moment, I think about the girls who will be tortured and killed, but needing to focus on finding Eden, I climb back into the helicopter.

As the aircraft lifts into the sky, I stare out the window at the vast ocean, worried I might not get to my woman in time.

Damiano's phone starts to ring, drawing my attention to him. I watch as he takes the device out and how his expression relaxes for a split second.

"I'm busy…No…No…"

Angelo and I stare at Damiano as we watch him on the call because that's one 'no' too many for a man who only says it once before killing you.

"No…No…I know…Christ, I don't have time for this," he finally snaps. "Don't call again."

He hangs up, the frown on his forehead instantly turning darker.

"Who was that?" Angelo asks.

"No one," Damiano mutters. "Carlo, take us back to land."

"We don't have a choice," Carlo mumbles. "We need to fuel up if we're going to continue searching."

"I need to get to my system at my place," I say. "We're wasting time out here."

Eden

I'm sitting on the floor, with my back to the wall where the other four women are standing.

The one with the blank stare whispered something in a language I've never heard, but it sounded like a prayer.

God. It's me. Eden. Your least favorite child, seeing as you keep dumping shit all over me. If you're listening, I'd really appreciate a break right about now.

I lift a hand and brush my fingers lightly over the bruises on my face and the massive bump on my head that feels like it's the size of an egg.

When I came to, the man with the gun was gone, and so was the body. There's blood on the floor, and I keep staring at it.

The door opens, and two armed men come in. They gesture with huge machine guns for us to come.

Where? Why?

Shit.

"Let me go," one of the women starts to cry. "Please."

My eyes dart between her and the men as I climb to my feet. I'm hit with a dizzy spell that makes the bile in my stomach churn.

One of the men aims his weapon at her and barks, "Shut the fuck up and come so you can piss and drink water."

My body begins to tremble violently, and not wanting to die right here, I walk toward the door while keeping an eye on the men.

When I step into the hallway, there's another armed man who nods for me to go into a restroom.

"Please," I hear the other women beg, and I brace myself to hear a shot being fired. My skin tingles, and the trembling in my body gets worse.

"Leave the door open," the man in the hallway orders. "Don't try anything stupid."

Walking into the small restroom, I have some cover behind a wall. I quickly relieve myself before drinking as much water as I can handle. God knows when we'll get something to drink again.

When I step into the hallway, I'm grabbed by my arm and shoved back into the room. Stumbling, I manage to keep my balance while shooting the asshole a glare.

Minutes later, the door is locked again, and the woman who was begging begins to cry hysterically.

Walking to the window, I look outside, trying to see where we are. It's night again, but my eyes widen when I can make out a dock and various types of boats.

We're not at sea anymore.

I keep standing by the window until I notice it's starting to get light outside. When it feels like hours are passing with no one coming to the room, I sink down to the floor and pull my knees up to my chest.

Surely, they won't keep us here for much longer?

None of the women are talking to each other, and when the silence starts getting to me, I say, "My name is Eden. What's yours?"

The one who was crying hysterically whispers, "I'm Milania."

The other three remain quiet, making me think they're traumatized out of their minds.

"Hi, Milania." I try to offer her a smile. "How did you get on the boat?"

"I was told there was work in New York. I paid two hundred and fifty dollars, and when I was picked up in Miami, I was brought here. That was many days ago. They keep drugging us."

"It's so we'll fuck for drugs," the one with the blank stare suddenly murmurs in a monotonous tone.

Glancing down at the two bruises on my arm, I gently rub my fingers over them.

There's no way I'll get addicted. I'm not Mandy.

I lift my head, and climbing back to my feet, I look out the window again, but it's quiet on the part of the dock I can see.

I wrap my arms around myself, and as the reality of my dire situation really sets in, destructive emotions fill my chest.

What does Dario think happened to me?

Poor Tyrone. He must be beside himself with worry.

I hope Quincy survived.

I suck in a shaky breath as my eyes start to blur with unshed tears.

I'm not going to let them turn me into a junkie who'll do anything for a hit.

I refuse.

I'd rather die.

None of my tears fall as I keep staring out the small window.

After a while, I sit down again and hug my knees to my chest. The cold is getting to me. It feels as if it's creeping into my very bones.

I struggle to process the hopeless emotions and to come up with a plan. But what can I do? Just like the other four women, I'm stuck. I have nothing I can use as a weapon.

A hell of a lot of time passes where nothing happens, and it starts driving me crazy.

Freezing my ass off, I climb to my feet and start to jog on the place so I can try and warm up a little.

"I'm scared," Milania whispers. A sob sputters from her, and she starts to cry again.

The exercise isn't helping shit, and stopping, I walk to Milania's side and sit down beside her. Lifting my arm, I wrap it around her.

I'm also scared.

I don't say the words out loud, though. Instead, I just hold her while she cries, my eyes locked on the small oval window.

I wonder what Dario's doing. Is he worried because I disappeared on him?

Tyrone is probably creating a scene at the police station, but they won't do shit. When people like us disappear, no one cares.

No one's going to look for me.

The thought hits hard, and it takes everything I have not to burst out in tears.

Jesus, I've finally found some happiness. I had a good thing with Dario. Yeah, money wasn't great, but I'm used to that. I had Dario and Tyrone, two amazing men who cared about me.

I had love.

I shake my head in an attempt to stop the morbid thoughts, and letting go of Milania, I get up again. When I look out the window, I notice it's gotten dark.

The assholes have left us in here all day long.

I walk to the door and turn the doorknob, but it's locked.

They can at least give us something to eat and drink. Another toilet break would be very welcome right about now.

Not caring whether I'll get in trouble, I bang a fist on the door. "Hey. Open the door." Bang. Bang. Bang. "Anyone there? Open! I need to pee."

"You're going to get in trouble," Milania whispers.

When no one comes to open the door, I stop and scowl at the piece of wood that's keeping me imprisoned in this freezing room.

An idea pops into my head, and I walk to the other side of the room before breaking out into a run and throwing my shoulder and side into the door, hoping I can break it open.

The door doesn't budge.

I, on the on the other hand, bounce backward before landing flat on my ass, my shoulder and hip aching.

Well, that didn't go as planned.

Before I can climb to my feet, I hear the lock turn, then the door opens.

I scramble up as the two armed men from earlier come in, and again, they gesture to the door. "Move."

Yeah, I don't need to be told twice.

My ass is out the door, and I walk toward the steps.

If I thought the room was cold, I'm in for a frigid surprise as I take the steps up to the deck, and the evening winter wind hits me square in the face and chest.

"J-Jesus." My teeth start to clatter, and I wrap my arms around myself as my body shivers uncontrollably.

I'm grabbed by the arm, and because I'm half frozen, the biting hold the man has on me hurts like a motherfucking bitch.

"Y-you're h-hurting m-m-me," I mutter, my breaths becoming mere huffs of white air.

"Shut up," he grumbles.

He hauls my ass off the boat and onto the deck, and I'm forced to walk toward another van wearing only my panties and bra.

They keep moving us, which will make it so much harder for anyone to find me.

That's if there's even someone looking.

Which I doubt.

Chapter 25

Dario

It's been over thirty-six hours since Eden was taken, and I'm starting to lose my mind.

I've just called Mrs. Stafford and asked her to check in on Quincy. When she asked what happened, I told her I had no idea.

I can't deal with the ballet company right now, and she'll have to run everything in my absence.

All I can think about is Eden.

I'm sitting in my office and staring at useless information.

A phone ringing draws my attention, and I glance at my jacket that's still lying on the floor where I threw it after I took it off.

Getting up, I dig Eden's phone out, and seeing Tyrone's name, I answer, "Hi."

"I'm losing my mind over here," he whimpers, the heartache and worry making his voice sound much deeper. "I need to know something."

I close my eyes. "I have nothing yet. I'm still looking."

"But you're the mafia. You can do shit. Right?"

I glance at the monitors where information is popping up all over, but there's nothing of use to me.

"I'm looking for her, Tyrone," I say, hoping it will ease his worry a little. "I won't stop until I find Eden. I promise."

The giant man chokes up, and I have to clench my teeth because my own emotions are all over the place. I'm up to my neck in worry, and my fucking heart is crumbling in my chest.

"I'll find her," I repeat the words more for myself than for Tyrone.

"Okay. Call me if you hear anything. Please."

"I will."

When he doesn't hang up, I end the call. I place the device next to mine and stare down at the two cell phones.

Mine is brand new, and Eden's looks like it's been to hell and back.

I need to get her a new phone.

The thought robs the air from my lungs because I might not get the chance.

Thirty-six hours is a fucking long time. She could already be dead.

I suck in a painful breath, then my breathing speeds up. It feels as if my heart is slamming against my ribs.

She's not dead.

I hear movement behind me, and turning around, I expect to see one of the guys, but it's Esmerelda. The woman who raised me shuts the door so we'll have privacy before coming to wrap her arms around me.

She doesn't say anything because we've been here before, and we both know words won't help.

It takes me a moment before I return her hug. The instant I do, the emotions, I've done my best to control, erupt like a volcano.

I grip Esmerelda tighter as my body shudders from the force of worry and heartache hitting me.

My housekeeper starts patting my back like she did when I was younger, and I almost break down and cry like a fucking toddler.

Unable to give in to the tears, I push her away and take a seat behind my system.

While my eyes flit over the monitors, I rein in my out-of-control emotions and force myself to focus.

Eden needs me.

"Can I bring you something to eat?" Esmerelda asks in a soft tone.

I shake my head. "Just take care of Bella and the other men."

I hear the door open, and sucking in a deep breath, I begin to search every corner of the dark web.

Even though I know Eden was on a boat, I keep running facial recognition, hoping she'll pop up again.

Eden

I have no idea where we are when the van comes to a stop.

I'm cold and about to pee right where I'm sitting.

The doors open, and the icy wind blows over our bodies.

At this rate, we're going to freeze and starve to death.

Armed men haul us out of the van, and I quickly glance around, noticing we're in a neighborhood. We're ushered into a house that's seen better days.

Are we back in Brownsville?

Nah. All the boats and shit just to come back here? That's overkill.

As soon as we're in the house, I mutter, "I need to pee." When the men ignore me, I snap, "I swear I'll piss right here."

We're shoved down a hallway and brought to a standstill outside a doorway.

"One at a time," one of the assholes barks.

I'm shoved into a restroom, but as I turn to shut the door, the asshole shakes his head and snaps, "Piss or hold it in."

"Jesus," I mutter as I go to the toilet. With a fucking audience, I push down my panties and sit. While I relieve my bladder, I keep glaring at the motherfucking bastard for not giving me privacy.

When I'm done, I give him a daring look as I take a moment to open the faucet by the sink. I cup my hand beneath the cold spray and drink some water.

Leaving the restroom, I shake the extra drops off my hands.

When all of us are done using the toilet, one of the men orders, "Into the room." He gestures with the barrel of his gun to another doorway.

I'm first to enter the room furnished with two shitty beds with thin, stained mattresses.

This place makes my apartment look like a mansion, which is saying a lot.

My eyes land on a bunch of ratty blankets, and not giving a shit that they might be flea infested, I rush forward and grab one. Wrapping the scratchy fabric around my frozen body, I side-eye the filthy beds while sitting down on the worn carpet.

The other women also grab blankets and find a spot against the wall.

When the men come in, my eyes lock on them, watching their every move.

Acting braver than I feel, I ask, "Are we going to get food?"

They ignore my question, and when one of them grabs the glazed-eye woman's arm, and the other pulls out an injection, I shout, "Hey. Leave her alone!"

I climb to my feet, and not sure what to do, I watch as they inject her with drugs with a horrifying sinking feeling in my gut.

No. Fuck that shit.

Keeping the blanket around me, I make a run for it.

"Come back here!" an asshole hollers.

I make it to the front door and yank it open. My feet hit the cold cement of the porch, and I fly down the stairs.

The blanket flutters around me like a cape as I hightail it over the yard and down the street.

I hear a bang, but nothing happens. Still, I push myself to run faster than I ever have, letting go of the blanket and only thinking about survival.

I have no idea whether the men are coming after me or letting me go.

My eyes dart wildly around me for a place where I can find safety. I don't bother with the houses because no one will open up. In neighborhoods like this, it's everyone for themselves.

I make it to a crossing, and not caring that cars are on the road, I dart across to the other side, reaching a business area.

Suddenly, the van swerves in front of me, coming to a standstill half parked on the sidewalk.

I change direction to run around the vehicle, but one of the men jumps out the driver's side and grabs hold of my neck. I'm yanked to the side and slammed hard into the van.

Pain dazes me, and before I can recover, there's a punch to my ear, disorientating me completely.

As I begin to sink to the floor, the guy hauls me over his shoulder. I hear a door slide open, then I'm thrown onto the steel floor.

Letting out a groan, my head feels like it's going to split open.

My vision is blurry and sounds come and go before I lose consciousness.

Chapter 26

Dario

I roll my shoulders to ease the tension in them while my fingers keep flying over the keyboard.

"You've been at it for hours," Renzo mutters behind me. "Take a break."

"I'm fine."

No, I'm not.

It feels as if everything we've done to this point is a waste of time.

Letting out a frustrated growl, I slam my fist down on the fucking keyboard. Standing up, I grab the two cell phones and stalk out of the office before I smash my system to pieces.

"Hey," Renzo says as he comes after me. "You're doing everything you can."

I don't reply as I take the stairs down to where the rest of the men are crowding my apartment.

Damiano's sitting on one of the couches, busy on a call while side-eyeing Bella, who's lying beside him.

"I don't give a shit…no deal," he growls into the line.

I pick up Bella and shove her into Renzo's arms as I mutter, "I don't trust Damiano with my baby."

My comment draws a chuckle from some of the men, but then Damiano grumbles, "I already have your family. If you hurry, you can watch me kill them."

He ends the call, then rises to his full height, his dark eyes locking with mine. "Find anything?"

I shake my head. "Nothing we can use. You?"

"Just spoke to Miguel. He claims his men didn't take your woman, and another group that's operating in Brownsville is responsible."

His eyes flick to Bella, and I'm surprised when he pets her head.

Letting out a sigh, he carries on talking. "It doesn't matter which group took her. By now, they could've sold her to get the money owed to them. It's either that or she'll be forced to work the debt off."

My frustration and worry spike, and I snap, "We know that already."

Suddenly the alarm on my phone sounds, and I quickly look at the screen. Seeing there's been a match for Eden on a camera, I turn around and run back up the stairs. Bursting into my office, I grab a seat and enter the alert. It's a clear image of Eden crossing a road.

Christ.

My woman's alive.

Everything inside me stills as I stare at her terrified face.

It registers that she's in underwear and barefoot.

In the fucking cold.

I suck in a harsh breath as I keep staring at her, then all at once, every destructive emotion I've felt since she was taken floods back.

A roar is torn from my chest as I shoot to my feet. Grabbing the chair, I throw the fucking thing against the wall.

The other men come rushing one by one into the office.

Renzo grabs my shoulder as I turn back to my system, and when my eyes land on the photo of Eden again, out in the fucking freezing cold wearing only underwear, the need to destroy everything overwhelms me.

Franco darts in front of me before I can get to the system.

"Breaking shit isn't going to help," he says. "Deep breaths."

"You have proof she's alive," Renzo adds.

"Dario," Damiano's voice lashes through the air.

I suck in heavy breaths as the rage calms enough for me to think straight.

"Track that photo," Damiano orders.

Franco gives me a cautious look as he moves out of my way.

"I'm okay," I manage to breathe before I step closer to the desk and bring up a map of the area where the photo was taken.

Queens come up, and then it zeroes in on a crossing in Jamaica.

"She's only thirty minutes away," I mutter in disbelief.

She's been right here all along and not at fucking sea.

The other four come closer to the monitors, and I bring the map up on the largest screen so we can see it clearly.

"How long has it been since the alert came through?" Damiano asks.

I check and mutter, "Ten minutes."

"Carlo," he calls out.

"Boss?"

"Take men to this location," he points at the map and photo of Eden, "and search the area around it for that woman."

"On it, boss."

I start typing on the keyboard to see if she's been spotted elsewhere, but when nothing comes up, I grab my phone, shove it in my pocket, and hurry out of the office.

"Let the men look, Dario," Damiano calls out.

"No. I need to be out there," I mutter.

"Christ." I hear him curse.

When I get to the elevator, I slam the button and glance at my friends following after me.

"You can stay. I'll do this on my own," I say before I slam the button again.

"We're coming," Renzo replies.

The doors finally fucking open, and we pile inside. On the ride down, it's hard to stand still, and when we reach the basement, I shoot out and jog to my SUV.

"I'll ride with him," Renzo calls out.

"Let us know if you get any new information," Damiano orders.

Renzo climbs into the passenger seat while I slide behind the steering wheel. As I steer the SUV out of the parking area, I already start to feel a bit better, knowing I'm on my way to where Eden was last seen.

There's a good chance she's still in the area. She might be at a police station already.

"Call one of your contacts in law enforcement and have them check police stations in Queens," I tell Renzo.

"Good idea. She'd probably go there for help."

Checking the rearview mirror, I see the other SUVs behind me.

I'm actually surprised Damiano's coming along for the ride. Sure, he's always there to back us in a gunfight, but not when it comes to searching for someone.

When Renzo ends the call he made, I ask, "What do you think is up with Damiano?"

"What do you mean?"

"Usually, he considers things like this a waste of his time," I explain. "But he's been with us since Eden was taken."

Renzo shoots a frown my way. "Because you need him."

When I give my friend a confused look, he explains, "We're all here because every single time shit went down in our lives, you were front and center to help us. You're the fucking heart of the Cosa Nostra, brother."

Christ.

Feeling overwhelmed by what Renzo just said, I keep my eyes focused on the road.

"You can cry," he teases me. "I won't tell anyone."

"Fuck off," I mutter, the corner of my mouth lifting slightly.

Renzo's phone starts ringing, and while he's on the call, I take a few deep breaths and focus on the mission.

He ends the call, then mutters, "My contact says there was a report of a woman being forcefully shoved into a van. It sounds like it could be Eden. The witness said the van's brown."

"Fuck," I growl, slamming my hand against the steering wheel. "If they got her again…"

"Just drive, Dario. At least we know to be on the check out for a brown van."

"Let the other's know about the van," I mutter.

"On it."

Renzo quickly sends out a group text, and when we reach the neighborhood in Queens where Eden was spotted, we start driving up and down streets.

On every other street, we drive by a vehicle with mafia soldiers. With such an overwhelming presence in the neighborhood, I start to have hope that one of us will spot the brown van.

Just as I turn by a crossing, Renzo's phone rings.

"It's Franco," he says before putting the call on speakerphone.

"What's up?" Renzo mutters.

"I've just driven past a house with a brown van. I'm parked up the street. Want me to wait or go in?"

"Send the address," I say. "Wait for us to get there."

"Okay."

The call ends, and the address comes through a few seconds later. Making a U-turn, I floor the gas.

Please let her be in that house.

I can't take any more of this and just want Eden back.

Chapter 27

Eden

(*After she was captured…again…*)

Lying on the floor, I struggle to keep my eyes open.

My head hurts so much.

I'm cold.

Through blurring vision, I see Milania crying. The other's just stare at random spots, no life on their faces.

I was so close to escaping.

That might've been my only chance.

I feel a needle prick my skin, and seconds later, my pain starts to fade.

No. I'd rather take the pain.

I blink and blink as the drugs rush through my system. Time warps, and everything feels upside down. My mind grows fuzzy until it feels like I'm floating.

When it looks like the beds are moving across the floor before jerking back into position, I frown because it's weird.

Something crawls over me, and I try to rub it off, but moving is difficult as if I'm restrained.

I'm tied up again. No!

I struggle, but I can't free myself, and more bugs are crawling over me.

I scream and fight the restraints, then suddenly, the restraints are gone, and Mandy's sitting in front of me, brushing her hand over my hair.

"It's easier when you just give up," she says.

Mandy never gave me a stitch of love or any kind of attention, so seeing her looking at me with worry makes something twist in my chest.

Stop. Don't touch me.

"It's okay," she coos. "We're family."

She lies down beside me so we're face-to-face and continues to stroke my hair, an unnaturally soft smile around her mouth.

I stare at Mandy's face, taking in all the lines and scars.

All my life, she's looked like this. Old. Tired. Shot up.

Bubbles form around her mouth, some floating into the air. Suddenly, she begins to convulse, and her eyes roll back into her head.

Staring at the white of her eyeballs is freaky as fuck, and I pinch my eyes shut.

When I open them again, Mandy is gone. Instead, Milania is lying beside me. Her eyes are frozen, and there's puke running from the corner of her mouth.

No.

I fight through the effects of the drugs and manage to lift my head, but it starts to throb.

I take hold of Milania's shoulder, and shaking her, my words are slurred as I say, "Get up. You need to sit up."

As my senses steadily return and the effects of the drugs wear off, the pungent stench of vomit hits me.

"Milania," I whisper.

Sitting up, I lean over her and try to check for her pulse, but I'm not sure I'm doing it right. I hold my finger beneath her nostrils, but there's no warm air coming from her.

"Shit," I whimper.

Hit with intense fear and sorrow all at once, I quickly move away from her.

She's dead.

Jesus, Milania's dead.

Lifting a hand, I cover my mouth while my breaths burst from me in quick, short puffs.

The warped hallucinations I had while high start to bombard me.

Milania died while I was high out of my mind.

I find a corner and hug my knees to my chest. "Jesus," I groan, rocking my body. "Jesus."

My face crumbles as I stare at her lifeless body, but no tears fall.

That's going to happen to me if I don't get out of here.

I press my face to my knees, but it hurts, and I have to lift my head again. I suck in deep breaths, the bile in my stomach churning and threatening to come up.

My eyes dart around the room, and I realize the one with the blank stare is gone. The other two are huddled beneath blankets, fast asleep.

I shake my head, struggling to process everything.

Needing to escape, I climb to my feet, using the wall as support. My head spins, and I feel queasy as fuck.

Don't puke.

Move.

When I reach the door, I peek up and down the hallway, and not seeing anyone, I sneak out of the room. I hear sounds coming from a TV, then someone lets out a loud burp.

"Get me another beer," a man orders.

"I'm not your fucking maid," another guy grumbles.

As I near the living room, I keep my body pressed against the wall, sucking in anxious breaths.

I can see part of the TV and boots resting on a coffee table. There's a window that has yellow-stained sheer curtains.

My eyes latch onto the front door, and my heart beats faster as I hype myself up to make a run for it.

Get to the door. Open it. Don't fuck up like they do in horror movies. Run like hell.

Movement catches the corner of my eye, and as I glance out the window again, I see armed men approaching the house.

Quite a few of them.

Shit. Shit. Shit. Shit.

The last thing I need right now is to be stuck in a gang war.

God, then it's game over for all of us.

The next second, the front door flies into the house as it's kicked in. Shocked out of my ever-loving mind, I watch as Dario comes in, looking like an avenging angel who's a second away from losing his mind.

"Holy shit," I mutter, completely stunned.

Wearing sexy-as-hell black cargo pants, and a sweater that spans tight across his chest, the man looks freaking hot.

His eyes, filled with rage, touch on me for a second as he raises his arms, a gun in each hand.

Holy shitballs, batman.

I tilt my head, wondering if I'm still hallucinating from the drugs as I watch him fire shot after shot in the direction where the men who are holding us captive are sitting.

Renzo comes in, followed by Franco, both looking as badass as Dario.

Confused out of my mind, I can only stand and stare, not sure what's real and what's not.

Renzo points his gun at me, and I start to shake my head. When he fires a shot, a squeak escapes me while I squeeze my body harder against the wall.

I glance down, searching for the bullet wound, but I don't find any. Hearing a groan behind me, I glance over my shoulder and see a man lying in the middle of the hallway.

The woman with the blank stare is standing in the doorway of the bedroom we were held in.

Jesus. Was she with that man?

I don't have time to think about it because I'm grabbed by my shoulders and squashed against a warm, solid chest.

"Fuck," Dario whispers. "Christ, Eden." He presses his face into my hair, rubbing his jaw over the bump on my head.

When I flinch and yank away from the pain, his hands move back to my shoulders, and he leans down so he can see my face.

His eyes flick all over my face while his own turns darker with anger.

His tone is harsh as he asks, "Are you okay?"

Am I?

"They drugged me," I complain, very upset about it. "I think four times."

"Let's go!" Franco snaps.

Dario slips his arms beneath me, and a second later, I'm lifted into the air and carried bridal style toward the front door.

If it weren't for the dead bodies in the living room and hallway, and Milania dying, and the fuck ton of shit I've been put through, this would actually be the most romantic moment of my life.

My eyes land on the woman with the blank stare, and it has me saying, "There are other women."

"The police will take care of them," Dario replies, still looking like the god of thunder as he carries me out of the house. "We need to get out of here."

I'm bundled into the back of an SUV, and Dario slides in beside me.

Renzo throws a coat at us while muttering, "Put this on her. She must be fucking freezing."

As soon as Dario shuts the door, he reaches for me again, and pulling me onto his lap, he tucks the coat around me.

His arms engulf me, and his scent fills my lungs.

"I'm taking her to our clinic," Renzo informs us from behind the steering wheel.

Dario can only make a growling sound in response to what Renzo said.

He pushes me slightly back so he can look at me, and as his eyes touch on all the bruises on my face and body, he becomes even angrier.

This is a side of him I didn't know existed.

I'm still trying to tie my boyfriend, who loves ballet and opera, to this badass, gun-wielding, hotter-than-ever man.

Lifting my hand, I press my palm against his chest. "Are you really here, or am I hallucinating?"

"I'm here, *Tesoro*."

His eyebrows draw together, the expression on his face bordering on heartbreaking as he keeps looking at me.

I move my hand to his jaw and whisper, "I'm okay. A bit frozen and roughed up, but okay."

He presses a kiss to my palm before I'm gently engulfed in his arms.

The love I feel coming from Dario chases the chill in my bones and warms my heart.

Chapter 28

Dario

I've just spent the last few hours impatiently waiting for the doctor to do all kinds of tests on Eden. His biggest worry was the blows she took to her head.

He wants to keep her overnight for observation because she has a concussion. She was allowed to take a warm shower, and dressed in a hospital gown, she's finally in bed with warm blankets covering her.

Sitting on the side of the bed, I keep staring at the bruises on her face. She has a busted lip, a purple shadow over her jaw, and a cut above her eye that's all the colors of the rainbow.

She looks at me with confusion in her eyes, but she hasn't asked any questions.

"Renzo went to get Tyrone. They'll be here soon," I mention.

"Thanks," she whispers, her gaze not leaving my face.

She takes a deep breath then chuckles. "So, what are you? A spy or some CIA agent?"

I shake my head. "The opposite."

Her eyebrows start to lift, but she stops when it tugs at the cut on her forehead.

"The opposite?" Her gaze darts over my face again. "A criminal?"

I brace myself for the worst before I nod. "The Cosa Nostra."

This time, the cut doesn't stop her eyebrows from flying into her hairline as she gasps, "Mafia?"

"He's one of the heads of the Cosa Nostra," Damiano suddenly says from behind me. "And because of it, he was able to save your life."

"I've got this," I mutter. I don't think Eden can handle Damiano right now.

"I'm his boss," the fucker says as he comes to take a seat on a chair. "I have questions."

Fucking robot.

"This can wait," I snap at him.

He only flicks his eyes in my direction before looking at Eden again.

When she begins to sit up, I shake my head, very unhappy. "You need to rest."

"I can answer a few questions," she argues. Folding her legs beneath her, she looks Damiano dead in the eye. "What do you want to know?"

"Who did you see, and what names did you hear?"

"I think there were four or five men when I was grabbed from the lobby."

"They're all dead," I mutter.

Surprise flashes over her face. "Oh." After she takes a deep breath, she continues, "I was out of it for a while, and when I came to, I was on a boat with different men. Obviously, seeing as you just said you killed the first lot."

She's quiet for a while, staring at a spot on my chest, then she shakes her head lightly as if she's coming out of a daze.

"I was transferred to a bigger boat and held in a room. There were armed men. When they tore off my dress, I killed one with my shoe."

The fuck?

"You took out an armed man with a shoe?" Damiano asks, actually sounding impressed.

"It's all I had. I buried the heel in his eye," she mumbles, her fingers twisting in the fabric of the covers.

"She can be your bodyguard, Dario," the fucker says. "Continue, Eden."

"I never heard any names. We were kept on the boat for a day before being moved to the house."

"Did you see tattoos?" Damiano shoots another question her way.

She thinks for a moment, then answers, "They wore warm clothes, but one of the men had a leaf on his neck with an M."

Damiano rises to his feet and surprises the fuck out of me when he comes to give Eden's shoulder a squeeze.

"You did good, Eden. Get some rest." Turning his attention to me, he says, "I'll give you a day to be with her, then you have to get to work. I want Miguel found."

"Got it," I reply and watch as he leaves the room.

"Miguel?" Eden asks, her tone soft.

"The drug dealers who took you work for him," I explain.

She nods, her eyes locking on my chest. Her features tighten, giving me the impression she's nervous.

"You okay?"

She nods again. "So…" Her tongue peeks out and brushes over the cut on her lip. "You're in the mafia."

"Yes." Needing to be open with her, I explain, "I take care of all the hacking and tracking jobs. I'm also a sniper for the family."

My body tenses as I wait for her to say something else.

When she remains quiet, I murmur, "Say something."

Her eyes lift to my face, and I watch as they shine with a look of wonder.

"A while back, when I asked if you have a dark side, this didn't cross my mind." She lets out an awkward-sounding chuckle. "When you came into the house all guns blazing I was shocked."

I'm surprised when Eden climbs onto my lap, and I quickly wrap my arms around her just happy she's not telling me to take a hike.

She tilts her head as she stares into my eyes again. "You were totally badass. It was hot."

My eyebrows draw together. "You're not angry that I kept it from you?"

She shrugs. "We both had our secrets. Besides, I've just been through hell. If you hadn't come for me, I'd still be there." She places her palms against my jaw and presses a soft kiss to my mouth. "And I've always had a thing for bad boys."

A grin forms on my face, and lifting a hand, I gently tuck some of her damp strands behind her ear.

"So we're good?" I ask.

She nods before snuggling into my chest, then I hear her whisper, "I just want you to hold me. The past two days were horrible."

I move us into a more comfortable position and lie down on the bed with my woman sprawled half over me. Keeping my arms wrapped around her, I drop kisses to her hair.

"Do you want to talk about it?" I ask.

She shakes her head and holds tighter onto me.

Just as some of the tension starts to leave my body, I hear hurried footsteps. The next second, Tyrone bursts into the room.

"Is she okay?!" he asks, his eyes locking on Eden.

We sit up again, and I move out of the way so he can get to her.

The mountain of a man swallows Eden in a hug, then a sob escapes him as he groans, "Jesus, baby girl. What they do to you?" He looks at the bruises on her face, then snaps, "The motherfuckers." Rubbing his hand up and down her back, he mutters, "Tyrone's here. It's gonna be okay."

"I was so scared I'd never see you again," she whimpers.

"Me too, baby girl." He lets out a heavy sigh. "Me too."

They hold each other for a while, and when the heavy emotion begins to subside, Tyrone looks at me and whispers, "Thank you."

I nod, and shoving my hands into my pockets, I watch as they hold each other for a little longer.

Eden is the first to pull back. She tries to smile, but her busted lip stops her.

"I'm okay. Just a couple of bumps and bruises," she says to put Tyrone at ease.

"The doctor's just keeping her overnight because she has a concussion. We can take her home tomorrow morning," I mention, seeing as I have to discuss something important with them.

"You'll need to bring me some clothes," Eden tells Tyrone.

"Okay."

"Actually, you need to pack enough clothes for a couple of weeks," I drop the bomb while locking eyes with Tyrone. "Eden's coming home with me, and because I know she'll be worried about you, I think it would be best if you stayed in one of my guestrooms."

"Why would I be worried?" Eden asks. "Do you think the drug dealers will come after me again and try to hurt Tyrone?"

I shake my head. "No. But we're going to war against Miguel's group, and I can't have you out there."

"Who's Miguel?" Tyrone asks.

"The fucker responsible for the drugs flooding Brownsville and the rest of New York," I answer.

Eden places her hand on Tyrone's forearm. "Will you come with me? Please?"

He inhales a deep breath before letting it out slowly. "Yeah. Anything for my baby girl."

She leans her head against his shoulder. "Thank you."

Happy that the conversation went well, I say, "Eden should get some sleep."

"I'll go pack our stuff. Want me to meet you here tomorrow?" Tyrone asks.

Digging my SUV's keys out of my pocket, I hand them to him. "There's an SUV parked out front. Take it. I'll text you my address. Once you're done packing, head over to my place. I'll notify my housekeeper that you're coming."

"Okay," he agrees. "I haven't driven in a while."

"It's okay." A smile curves the corners of my mouth. "The SUV is insured."

"I'll be careful," he assures me before nodding toward the doorway. "Can we talk alone?"

"Sure." I glance at Eden, who's crawling beneath the covers again. "I'll be right outside the door."

"Okay."

I follow Tyrone into the hallway, and when he turns to face me, there's a worried expression tightening his features.

"With you being in the mafia, will Eden be in danger?"

I shake my head. "No. I'll keep her safe." Knowing he needs to hear the words, I place my hand on his shoulder and say, "Eden is mine, and no one will dare lay a finger on her now that the word is out there. She has the full force of the Cosa Nostra protecting her."

He nods, then gives me a relieved smile. "Thanks for finding her and bringing her home."

Aware of the tight bond between Eden and Tyrone, I murmur, "I would've done the same if you were the one they took. You're important to Eden, which means you're important to me."

He lets out a chuckle. "Never thought I'd have a mafia boss say that to me."

Returning his smile, I mutter, "Yeah." I nod in the direction of the exit. "Get going, and don't take too long at the apartment. Grab what you need and get out of there."

Tyrone nods, but before he can walk away, I add, "Take my number so you can call me if something happens."

We quickly exchange numbers, and I send him my address.

He hesitates for a moment, then says, "Thanks for watching over us. You're good people, Dario."

I give him a chin lift, then watch as my future father-in-law walks down the hallway.

Chapter 29

Eden

I hear Dario's voice as he calls Esmerelda to let her know about Tyrone so she can get a room ready for him.

I didn't even argue when Dario said we'd be staying with him.

Why?

I'm still trying to find the answer when he comes back into the room.

Snuggled beneath the covers, I watch as he sits down on the armchair and removes his boots. Standing up, he pulls the two guns from behind his back. I'd forgotten they were tucked into his waistband.

He places them on the bedside table, and leaning over me, he presses a kiss to my temple, while whispering, "Move up, *Tesoro*."

I scoot back and lift the covers so he can climb beneath them. When he lies down, he wraps an arm around me and positions my body half over his.

Melting into the feel of his warmth, I let out a sigh.

This is why I didn't argue about staying with him.

I feel safe and loved.

He keeps giving me gentle hugs and pressing kisses against my hair.

"Want to talk?" he whispers.

"Yeah." I rub my good cheek against his chest. "It's hard to believe you're in the mafia. Is the ballet company a front for something?"

"No." I feel his warm breaths stir my hair as he adds, "I'm still the man who loves art, opera, and ballet." He pauses for a moment, then admits, "But I'm also a man who's killed. And I will kill again."

The memory of me slamming the heel of my shoe into that man's eye flashes through my mind.

"I've killed too," I whisper. "I have no idea what came over me. One second, I was fearing for my life, and the next, I was attacking them."

"And you managed to escape," he murmurs. "You're more badass than me."

"You know about my escape attempt?"

"Yes. I got the footage from a CCTV camera in the area. That's how we were able to figure out where you were."

A smile begins to curve my lips, but I stop when it tugs on the cut. "At least my escape attempt paid off."

Remembering what happened afterward, I hold Dario tighter and bury my face in the crook of his neck.

Milania.

"What's wrong?" Dario asks, concern lacing his words.

I suck in a deep breath of his scent, then say, "There was a woman with me. Milania. She died."

He presses another kiss to my hair. "I'm sorry, *Tesoro*."

"She was so scared. She kept crying," I whisper. "After they captured me again, we were given drugs. I had this crazy high where I saw Mandy, my mother, lying in front of me. We were face-to-face. When she started choking, it looked like the bubbles were floating."

My throat strains as all the harrowing shit I was subjected to overwhelms me. Letting out a sob, my voice is strained as I admit, "I did nothing while Milania died right in front of me because I thought she was Mandy."

"Shhh, *Tesoro*," he murmurs as he tightens his arms around me. "You were drugged. There was nothing you could do."

As my tears start to flow, there's no stopping them. Needing the release after the insane two days I've just been through, I cry my heart out against Dario's neck.

After a while, my emotions settle enough for me to stop crying, and feeling exhausted, I just lie still in his arms, hoping I'll fall asleep soon.

A nurse comes in to check on me, and when she asks how I'm feeling, I mutter, "Tired."

"Do you have a headache?"

"It's not as bad," I answer honestly.

She takes my vitals, then says, "Try to get some sleep."

I plan on doing just that.

Not wanting to think about everything that's happened, I focus on how good Dario smells and how amazing it feels to be in his arms.

This feeling is something I'll never take for granted.

I shift my head, resting my cheek on his chest again, and my eyes fall on the two guns.

Only then do I think to ask, "What kind of hospital is this that the nurse didn't say anything about the guns?"

"It's a clinic that belongs to the Cosa Nostra," he informs me.

"Oh." Remembering something, I ask, "Is everyone I met at the show in the mafia?"

"Yes." He starts to trail his fingers up and down my arm that's wrapped around his waist. "Renzo, Franco,

Angelo, and Damiano are the other four heads of the Cosa Nostra."

"And the women?"

"No, they're not involved in the organization."

When he brushes over the needle marks, my eyes latch onto them. The sight is disturbing, and it has me tensing.

Dario immediately notices and asks, "What's wrong?"

"I hate drugs." I swallow hard on the destructive feelings. "My mother is a drug addict, and I've seen what it's done to her. I've lived with it every day."

Shaking my head, I try to breathe through the tears that are threatening to fall.

My voice is strained as I whisper, "Now I have the same marks on my arm."

Dario's fingers wrap around the faded abrasions left by the cable ties on my wrist, and lifting my arm, he presses a kiss to each of the needle marks.

"They'll fade, *Tesoro*," he assures me.

"Yeah."

Silence falls between us, and I try not to think about the shit I've been through. I'll deal with everything tomorrow, but right now, I just want to sleep.

I move my head a little until I'm able to hear the steady beat of Dario's heart, and closing my eyes, I focus on the sound until I manage to drift off.

After I slept like the dead, I was checked by the doctor and cleared to go home.

Home, AKA Dario's penthouse.

I wonder how Tyrone reacted when he saw the place.

Probably the same as me, totally overwhelmed.

Earlier, Dario left to go and get his car and my clothes while I had breakfast.

Dario's a mob boss.

You'd think I'd be running for the hills, but here I am, sitting in the passenger side of his R8 as he drives us home.

Before shit went down, Dario was this perfect prince, and honestly, it bothered me a little. I didn't feel good enough to be with him.

But now…

I've seen his dark side, and in that moment when he killed the men holding me captive, I fell in love with him all over again.

Dario has blood on his hands. He's not as perfect as I first thought, but instead, he's perfect for me. He might be rich, and I'm okay with that, but we're no longer worlds apart, because we're both from the wrong side of life.

"What are you thinking about?" Dario asks, drawing me out of my thoughts.

Turning my head to look at the handsome man beside me, I admit, "How I fell in love with you all over again."

Surprise flickers over his face. "Yeah?"

"Yeah."

He steers the sports car into the basement and brings it to a stop in the designated parking bay.

Killing the engine he turns toward me, and carefully gripping my chin between his thumb and his forefinger, he presses a soft kiss to my mouth.

When he pulls back, he looks at me as if I'm his entire world, and it makes me feel like the luckiest woman alive.

If it weren't for Dario, I'd be…

I shake my head, and it makes a frown form on his forehead.

"What?" he asks.

"Just memories," I mutter before I shove the passenger door open.

Climbing out of the R8, I wait for Dario. He throws his arm around my shoulders and pulls me against his side as we walk to the elevator.

As soon as we're inside, Dario asks, "About the past two days?"

I nod, letting out a sigh.

"Would you like to see a therapist?"

The doors open, and as we step into the penthouse, I say, "No. I'm sure it will get better with time."

Bella barks and comes barreling toward us. Crouching down, I pick her up and pet her head as we walk through the foyer.

Tyrone comes from the direction of the kitchen. Seeing him in this luxurious place is weird as hell.

"Hey." I give him a small smile, careful not to tug at the cut.

He wraps me up in a tight hug, then asks, "How you feeling today?"

Like roadkill and off balance.

"Better."

Esmerelda also comes out of the kitchen, and seeing the state I'm in, she hurries to my side and takes hold of my arm.

"Dear God, we need to get you in bed. Come, child."

Not arguing, I let her drag me up the stairs to Dario's bedroom.

When she throws the covers back, there's a burst of warmth in my chest because I've never had a woman fuss over me before.

"Come. Get in. I'll make chicken soup. It's good for the soul," she mutters while nudging me to sit on the bed.

When she takes my sneakers off my feet, my eyebrows draw together, and I'm overcome with the urge to sob like a baby.

She straightens up, and noticing the emotion on my face, she sits down beside me and wraps an arm around my shoulders.

"There, there," she coos. "You're safe now. With a lot of rest, you'll be back to your usual self in no time."

I sniffle, and unable to stop the tears, they roll over my cheeks.

"I'll take over, Esmerelda," Dario says.

She lets go of me and leaves the room. Dario takes her place beside me, and the next second, I'm pulled onto his lap and squashed against his chest.

Just having him hold me gives me the strength to regain control over my emotions.

He calms me.

Resting my head against his shoulder, I close my eyes, and within seconds, I fall asleep in his arms.

Chapter 30

Dario

After Eden falls asleep, I lay her down on the bed and cover her with the blanket.

I quickly go to my office and place my weapons in the cabinet. Grabbing my laptop, I head back to the bedroom so I can watch over Eden while I work.

Careful not to wake her, I get comfortable on my side of the bed and open the device.

I have just as much interest in finding Miguel as Damiano has.

I have a couple of photos of the man, and uploading them all to my facial recognition app, I start the search for him.

Opening another program, I go into the dark web, offering a reward of one million dollars for whoever has information on the whereabouts of Miguel.

Done with that, I enter chat rooms and search for code words that drug dealers like to use. I spend the next couple of hours, sifting through shit, but I don't find anything we can use to our advantage.

Knowing Damiano will want an update, I dig my cell phone out of my pocket and send him a message.

Busy searching for Miguel. Will update you when I have news.

I set the phone to silent mode before placing it on the bedside table.

Glancing at Eden, I'm struck square in the chest by a wave of relief.

I have her back.

I place the laptop next to my phone, and lying down on my side, I stare at her sleeping face.

Christ, I'm never letting you out of my sight again.

I need to get her a tracker.

And guards.

I want her protected at all times.

Lifting my hand, I gently brush my fingers over her hair.

So this is what it feels like to love a woman with all my heart.

When she's in danger, there's only excruciating pain, and when she's close by and safe, there's a peaceful calmness.

My eyes drift over her face, touching on the bruises that look much worse today.

She's been through hell.

I wish I could wipe her memory.

I keep brushing my hand over her head, but then she starts to stir and mumbles, "Stop."

Pulling my hand away, I expect her to settle down again, but instead, her breathing speeds up, and she grips the pillow beneath her head, her body straining.

"NoNoNoNoNo." Her voice is tight with panic.

"*Tesoro*," I murmur, gently shaking her shoulder so she'll wake up.

"Stop!"

As the scream tears from her, I sit up in time to catch her when she darts up, her eyes opening wide. Horror bleeds over her face, making her look pale as fuck.

"It's just a dream," I say as I hold her close.

She shakes her head, her breaths not calming down. Her fingers grip the sweater I'm wearing tightly, her body trembling severely.

"You're safe." I begin to rock her, hoping it will help calm her. "I'm here, *Tesoro*. No one can get to you."

She clings to me, and minutes pass before her breathing returns to normal. She doesn't move but keeps still in my arms with her face buried against my chest.

Her tone sounds haunted when she whispers, "I hallucinated Mandy brushing her hand over my hair, but I think it was Milania."

Shit, I triggered her trauma.

"I'm sorry. I won't do it again."

"Huh?" She lifts her head and gives me a confused look.

"While you were sleeping, I caressed your hair, which must've triggered you," I explain. "Sorry, *Tesoro*."

"Oh." She tries to give me a brave smile, busted lip and all. "Don't worry. I'm okay."

Christ, this woman is incredible.

She catches me staring at her and asks, "Why are you looking at me like that?"

"I'm just thinking that you're the strongest, most beautiful woman I've ever met, and I'm one hell of a lucky man because you're mine."

"Yeah?" A smile tugs at her mouth, and moving onto her knees, she wraps her arms around my neck. "I'm yours?"

"Yes." Engulfing her in my arms, I stare into her gray eyes until I lose myself in them. "You're mine, Eden. I'm never letting you go."

She brings a hand to my face and brushes her fingers over my jaw.

Caught up in each other, my heart overflows with love for her, and for the first time in my life, I say the words to a woman.

"I love you."

Instead of looking happy, Eden's face starts to crumble, and a second later, she bursts out in tears.

I'm just about to haul her against my chest again when she looks at me through her tears.

"You have no idea how much hearing those words mean to me." She presses a kiss to my mouth. "That's all I ever wanted. Just to be loved for who I am."

Christ.

Hearing how much she needed to be loved makes me wish I had met her much sooner.

"I love you, Eden," I say again, my voice a little hoarse with emotion. "So fucking much my heart feels like it's going to burst."

She lets out a chuckle, and finally giving me a happy smile, she plasters herself to me. Near my ear, she whispers, "I love you too, baby."

Her declaration washes over me, calming the darkness that was unleashed in me over the past two days.

Our timing might've been off, but we both needed to hear the words that bind us together for life.

Lying down with Eden in my arms, I kiss her tenderly, careful not to hurt her.

Just as she lets out a needy moan, Esmerelda calls from the doorway, "Lunch is ready."

"Come on," I say, pulling Eden out of bed.

We head out of the room, and taking the stairs down, we're greeted by an excited Bella. I pick up my furball and rub her head as I walk to the kitchen.

Seeing Tyrone sitting by the island in the kitchen, already eating, a smile tugs at my mouth.

"Are you settling in okay?" I ask, opening the fridge to grab two beers.

"Yeah. Esmerelda's nice."

My eyebrow lifts when I see the interest in his eyes the second my housekeeper enters the kitchen.

Placing a beer in front of him, I say, "I know. She's like a mother to me."

"Am I not getting a beer?" Eden asks as she takes a seat by the island.

"No." I give her a pointed look. "You're still recovering."

I sit down beside her as Tyrone asks, "How you feeling, baby girl?"

"A little out of it." She waves a hand in the air. "I'll be fine tomorrow."

Esmerelda places two bowls of chicken soup in front of us, and it has me scowling. "I'm not sick."

"We all eat what Eden eats," she grumbles at me.

Just as I'm about to argue, she brings a stack of grilled cheese sandwiches.

"That's better," I mutter as I help myself to one.

My housekeeper sits down beside Tyrone and adds more sandwiches to his plate.

We eat in silence for a while, then Tyrone mentions, "You have a nice place, Dario. A bit big, but nice all the same."

"What was your reaction when you walked into the penthouse the first time?" Eden asks.

Tyrone just shrugs.

"He was a little overwhelmed," Esmerelda busts him. "He also called me ma'am like Eden did when we met."

"Felt like I was meeting royalty or some shit," Tyrone mutters.

As we continue to eat our food, I keep glancing at Eden, constantly needing to make sure she's next to me.

She doesn't eat as much as I had hoped she would.

She pushes her bowl away and smiles at Esmerelda. "Thanks for lunch. Can I help clean up?"

"No, that's my job," Esmerelda replies. "You can go back to bed and get more rest." She shoots me a serious look. "Don't keep her up."

"Yes, ma'am," I mutter before I finish the last of my sandwich.

Eden gets up and gives Tyrone's arm a squeeze before she leaves the kitchen with Bella trailing behind her.

As soon as she's gone, Tyrone locks eyes with me. "How's she really doing?"

I shake my head. "I'm not sure. She went through a lot, so it will take time for her to heal."

"Did she tell you what happened?"

I nod.

"Bad shit?" he asks, looking concerned.

Yeah, bad shit.

Getting up from my chair, I say, "I'll let her tell you when she's ready. Okay?"

"Should I be worried?"

I shake my head. "I don't think so. She's very strong."

"Yeah." He glances in the direction of the stairs. "She is."

"Thanks for the food," I tell Esmerelda before I leave the kitchen to check on Eden.

"You're welcome," she calls after me.

When I head up the stairs, I hear Tyrone say, "Let me help you. It will drive me crazy sitting around and doing nothing all day."

"Okay. That would be nice."

A smile tugs at the corner of my mouth, and when I walk into the bedroom, I let out a chuckle when I see Bella curled up next to Eden.

I could get used to seeing my woman in my bed.

Chapter 31

Eden

It feels like all I've done since Dario rescued me is sleep and eat.

I'm lying on the bed, staring up at the ceiling while Dario's working. At first, I tried to take an interest in what he was doing, but that shit's so far over my head I quickly gave up.

Suddenly, it hits me like a lightning bolt that I haven't called Sylvia, and I shoot upright into a sitting position. "Shit!"

The laptop almost flies off Dario's lap as he shoves it aside, and a second later, his arm's wrapped around my shoulder.

"What? Are you in pain?"

"I didn't call my boss. She's going to fire my ass."

Shit, I lost my phone when I was grabbed.

Dario gets up and leaves the room, which has me calling after him, "Can I use your phone?"

Less than a minute later, he comes back, and when I see my phone in his hand, I crawl to the edge of the bed, asking, "Is it charged?"

"Yes."

He hands it to me, and I quickly dial the diner's number. It takes a while before the call is answered.

"Ben's Burgers, how can we help you?" Sherrie's voice comes over the line.

"Hi, Sherrie, it's Eden."

"Oh my God! Where have you been? Sylvia's been losing her shit."

Where have I been?

Not ready to tell anyone, I lie. "I was mugged again. The guy beat me up, and I was out of it. Is Sylvia there? Can I talk to her?"

A frown forms on his forehead. "Again? There was a first time?"

Shit.

I indicate for him to wait as Sherrie says, "Girl, you have the worst luck. Hold on while I get her."

A moment later Sylvia's voice sounds up in my ear. "Sherrie said you were mugged again. You okay?"

"Just beaten up pretty bad. Sorry, I didn't call sooner."

"I almost advertised your job. You're lucky you called today. When will you be back? We're getting busy with the holiday rush."

Jesus.

"I'll be in tomo–"

Dario pulls the phone out of my hand, and taking over the conversation, he says, "This is Dario, Eden's boyfriend. She won't be in for at least two weeks." He listens for a moment, then mutters, "Do what you have to do."

When he hangs up the call, I stare at him with wide eyes.

He sets the phone down on the bed, and leaning over me, he grips my chin between his thumb and forefinger.

Locking eyes with me, he grumbles, "Things are going to change. You're no longer working at the diner. You will rest for the next two weeks."

When my lips part so I can argue with him, he shakes his head and gives me a firm look.

"You're my girlfriend, and that means I get to take care of you. It's not open for discussion. I understand you're a strong, independent woman, but it doesn't mean I'm going to stand by and watch you work yourself to death."

My lips part again, but he stops me from talking with another serious look while saying, "I'm not done yet."

Okay.

I'm liking this dominant side of him.

Dario sits down in front of me, moving his hand from my chin to the side of my neck.

"We have to meet in the middle, *Tesoro*. I won't keep you from working, but you have to let me do things for you. Starting with me buying you a new phone."

Looking at the man who's stolen my heart, I suppress the urge to argue. I know I can be stubborn, but I can't just think about myself anymore.

"It's going to be difficult," I admit. "I'm not used to taking things from people."

"I'm not people." He tilts his head. "I'm your boyfriend."

"What if I make all these changes, and you break up with me?" I ask the question that worries me the most.

Dario surprises the hell out of me when he says, "If it's security you need, I'll marry you tomorrow."

"Huh?"

I blink at the man as if he's lost his mind. When the words sink in, I start to laugh, shaking my head. "It's way too soon."

"Not for me."

Realizing he's serious, I gape at him. "Jesus, Dario. We've only dated for a few weeks. Marriage is a serious commitment."

"So?"

"Two weeks!" I give him an incredulous look.

With a dead serious expression, he mutters, "It doesn't matter whether we're dating or married because I'm never letting you go."

"We can talk about marriage at a much later stage," I say. Wiping a hand over my forehead, I mumble, "Now I've forgotten what we were talking about."

"You said you're scared of making changes and talked shit about us breaking up, then I brought up marriage, and you freaked out," he reminds me.

"Right." I let out a sigh, and feeling tired from the intense conversation, I lie down.

Dario crawls over me and bracing his hands on either side of my head, he locks eyes with me.

"You need security, and I want to give it to you. Let me transfer an amount into your bank account, so if the impossible happens and we break up, you'll have money while you figure out what to do."

"I can't just take your money," I mutter.

"I'll make you a deal," he says. "When you're better, you'll dance for me every night. Take the money as payment."

You need to meet him in the middle.

But damn, it's difficult.

Giving in, I nod. "Okay."

The corners of his mouth lift, and he presses a soft kiss to my mouth, then mutters, "Christ, you're a tough negotiator."

Bella wakes up from where she's snoozing, and worms her way in between Dario and me, sniffing all over my face.

Dario climbs off me, and a second later, says, "Give me your banking details."

I ramble the details to him while playing with Bella.

Dario lets out a chuckle as he opens his laptop again. "Just remember you agreed to the deal."

"Yeah-yeah." I sit up again. "I've slept enough. Can we watch some TV?"

"Give me a second while I wait for the transfer to go through."

"It could've waited." I climb off the bed and pick up my cell phone. Noticing I have messages I scroll through them.

There are two from Sylvia threatening me to get my ass to work, but they were sent before I called her.

There's one from Sherrie asking if I'm okay.

I open the text and send her a reply.

Thanks for checking up on me. I'll swing by the diner when I'm better.

Opening the last message, I let out a gasp.

Quincy: I don't know if you'll ever see this. I'm okay. I hope you're okay too. No one's telling me shit.

Jesus, how could I forget about him?

Pressing dial on his number, I don't have to wait long for him to answer.

"Eden! Are you okay? Where are you?"

Hearing the worry in his voice makes me feel a little emotional.

"I'm fine. I'm at home. Are you still in the hospital?"

"Nah, I got out this morning. I'm at home with Anita making a fuss over me."

I let out a relieved sigh. "I'm so happy to hear that." Brushing a hand through my hair, I mutter, "I'm sorry you got shot because of me."

He clears his throat. "What happened to you after they shot me?"

"Nothing worth retelling," I say so I won't cause him any worry. My chin starts to tremble, and I swallow hard on the emotion. "I'm glad you're home."

Dario comes to stand next to me, rubbing his hand up and down my back.

"I have to go, but it was nice talking to you," I tell Quincy. "Enjoy all the attention you're getting from Anita."

"I will. Take care of yourself."

We end the call, and I let out another breath of relief.

"Quincy?" Dario asks.

"Yeah." I glance up at him. "How did you know?"

"You mentioned hospital and Anita, which is his wife's name."

"Right."

"Come on. You can watch TV with Tyrone while I go out."

I pick up Bella, and walking out of the bedroom, I ask, "Where are you going?"

"To get a couple of things. I won't be too long."

When I get to the living room, I make myself comfortable on the couch and let Bella snuggle in my lap.

When Tyrone comes to sit with me, he says, "I've been told to guard you while your man goes out."

I let out a chuckle because no one needs to tell Tyrone to guard me. He's been doing it all my life.

Dario comes to kiss me goodbye, and as he leaves the apartment, I switch on the TV and pick a comedy to watch.

Chapter 32

Dario

"Dario," Eden gasps, looking shocked out of her mind. "You call this meeting me in the middle?"

I point at the phone and laptop. "You need those. Your phone is from the Middle Ages."

Tyrone lets out a chuckle, which earns him a scowl from Eden, then she gestures at the earrings and necklace set that I couldn't resist getting for her.

"I suppose you're going to tell me I need those too?" she asks.

I figured she'd be okay with them as long as she didn't know they cost thirty-eight thousand dollars.

"No, I got them because they'll look beautiful on you," I explain.

"They sure are sparkly," Tyrone adds his two cents. "Must've cost quite a bit."

"You're not helping," I mutter at him.

"Hey, I'm on her side." He points at Eden, who shakes her head while she waves a hand at the *Louis Vuitton* handbag.

I shrug. "It's just a handbag."

She waves her arm wildly over the *Dolce & Gabanna* wallet, the *Cartier* watch, and *Dior* perfume.

"I could've redone your entire wardrobe," I say in my defense.

"Jesus, you just love digging at that grave she's going to bury you in," Tyrone chuckles, getting way too much pleasure out of the shit I find myself in.

Esmerelda comes closer and looks at everything I bought. "It's not that much. I'm actually surprised there aren't car keys."

I wrap my arm around my housekeeper. "They're putting a bulletproof coating on the car."

"The what?" Eden gasps.

Letting go of Esmerelda, I walk closer to my woman and wrap my arms around her.

Locking eyes with her, I say, "It's just a few gifts, *Tesoro*. It would make me incredibly happy if you accepted them."

She lets out a sigh, and luckily for me, her features start relaxing as she whispers, "It's a lot."

I press a kiss to her left cheek. "No, it's not." I kiss her right cheek. "You deserve the world, and I want to give it to you."

"I'm going to my apartment," Esmerelda says. "Tyrone, care to join me for a cup of coffee?"

"We just had coffee," he replies.

"Come with me so they can have some privacy," she snaps at him, which has him shooting up from the couch.

"Yes, ma'am."

Eden and I watch as they leave the penthouse, then I turn my attention back to my woman.

"Please accept the gifts."

She glances at everything on the coffee table, then says, "Okay, but you don't have to buy me stuff."

"I do. It makes me feel good knowing I'm taking care of you. Let me spoil my girlfriend when and however I want."

Wrapping her arms around my neck, she finally relents. "Okay."

Excited, I let go of her and pick up the phone. "Want me to set it up for you?"

Eden lets out a chuckle as she sits down on the couch. "Please."

I switch the device on, and it takes a few minutes for me to sign Eden into all her apps. When I'm done, I hand it to her.

"Thank you," she whispers as she looks at the device in her hand before glancing at the other gifts.

When she's quiet for too long, I ask, "Are you okay?"

She nods, and gently brushing her fingers over the screen of her phone, she admits, "I've never had nice things like this before." She glances around the penthouse before looking at me. "It feels like I've been thrown into some kind of alternate universe. It's like a fairy tale, and I'm scared if I get used to it, it will be taken away from me."

"Never, *Tesoro*," I assure her. "This is your life now, and nothing can take it away from you, because I'll kill whoever dares to try."

The corner of her mouth lifts. "I keep forgetting you're in the mafia."

Leaning forward, she picks up the earrings. "They look so expensive. I'm scared to wear them."

"Put them on for me," I murmur.

Her smile grows as she slips them into the tiny holes in her earlobes, then she lets me help her with the necklace.

Getting up, she walks to the restroom, and not wanting to miss her reaction, I follow her.

When she stops in front of the mirror, she sucks in a deep breath as she stares at her reflection. "Jesus, the black eye looks even worse today."

"The bruises will heal." I stand behind her and place my hands on her hips. "The diamonds look perfect on you."

"Yesterday I thought it was game over for me, and today I'm wearing…" her voice cracks, and spinning around, she buries her face against my chest.

I hold my woman tightly as the trauma of her captivity hits, knowing this won't be the last time she breaks down.

When she regains control over her emotions, she mutters, "Sorry, I'm ruining the evening."

"You're not ruining anything." Pulling her out of the restroom, I lead her back to one of the couches. "Want me to make you some tea?"

"Please."

Sitting down, she takes off the pieces of jewelry and places them carefully back in their boxes.

I hurry to the kitchen and make her a cup of camomile tea. While I'm busy, I think about her strong reaction to the gifts.

"Jesus!" I hear Eden shout.

Leaving the tea, I rush back to the living room, only to find her staring at her phone.

Standing in the doorway, I say, "What?"

Her eyes are wide, and she seems a little pale.

Hurrying closer, I take hold of her hand and turn the phone so I can see what she's looking at.

Oh...Fuck.

Her bank balance.

"We had a deal," I remind her. "You agreed to it."

Then it registers that she only had twelve dollars before I transferred money into her bank account.

She grabs the phone and looks at her balance again before giving me a bewildered look.

"It's just money," I murmur.

Finally, she finds her voice. "It's...Jesus." She shows me the screen again. "Look closely. Did you make a mistake and type in too many zeroes? I can go to the bank tomorrow and send it back to you."

My eyebrow lifts, and grabbing her wrist, I tug her against my chest.

"Don't you fucking dare return any of it. That will piss me off."

She gapes at me as if I've lost my mind, then mutters, "It's way too much. It's...It's..."

"It's yours. We had this conversation already. You needed security."

"But..." Her eyebrows draw together. "It's a million dollars, Dario. A. Million. Dollars." Her eyes widen again. "Oh my God. One Million Dollars." Lifting a hand to her forehead, she begins to look a little queasy.

Picking my woman up bridal style, I take a seat on the couch and position her on my lap. I frame her face with my hands, and press a kiss to her parted lips.

"It's so much," she whispers.

"And not nearly enough." I give her a pleading look. "Let me give you the world, *Tesoro*."

"But..." she shakes her head. "Don't you need the money? I know you're rich, but I thought you had...like a couple of million, and if you give me so much, what does that leave you with? And how do I...? What do I...?"

I force her to look at me. "Breathe, *Tesoro*."

She inhales a deep breath, her gray eyes stormy with conflicting emotions.

"I have a hell of a lot more than a couple of million," I say so she won't worry about me. "To me, a million is like..." Remembering her balance before I sent her money, it's actually hard to think of an amount to compare it to, and I end up muttering, "It's nothing to me. I won't miss it at all, so please take it."

She stares at me for a long while before looking at her bank balance again.

I wait patiently until she murmurs, "What do I do with so much money?"

"Whatever you want." Pulling the phone out of her hold, I set it down on the table beside the couch before focusing all my attention on Eden again. "You can invest some."

"Yes. I have to get it out of my account before someone steals it."

"No one will steal it."

"You sure?"

"Yes. Besides, if someone is dumb enough to steal from you, I'll track the fucker down and get it back before killing him."

Her tongue darts out to wet her lips while her eyes search mine, then she asks, "Have you killed a lot?"

Lifting my hand, I brush a couple of strands behind her ear. "Do you really want to know?"

"The mafia is this whole other side of you that I don't know."

"As I've said before, I mostly take care of the hacking and tracking part of things. I'm also backup for the family, so if we have a meeting with another group, I'll be on a roof with my sniper rifle to take out any threats."

"Have you ever killed a regular person? You know, someone who isn't a criminal."

I shake my head.

She seems to relax a little, and it has me asking, "Feeling better?"

"Yeah." Leaning her head against my shoulder, she lets out a heavy breath. "It's just a lot to take in all at once."

"I know. I'm trying to take it slow, but after I almost lost you, it's difficult. I just want to love you in every way possible."

She turns on my lap until she's straddling me and meets my eyes. "I'm not going to lie, you're a hell of a lot more intense since the shit went down, but I get why." Leaning closer she presses a soft kiss to my mouth before giving me a beautiful smile. "Thank you, Dario."

"You're welcome, *Tesoro*."

Chapter 33

Eden

"So you basically fired me," I say, lifting my eyebrow at Dario, where he's standing in the doorway of his office.

"No. I got a replacement to work as a janitor at the ballet company because you need time to heal after the shit you went through."

"I've been off for a week. The bruises have faded a lot," I argue. "Besides, I work the night shift where no one actually sees me. I can go back to work."

He walks closer to me, and taking a deep breath, he says, "I'm not referring to the bruises, Tesoro. You need to process everything that happened to you."

"I'm much better." Taking hold of his hand, I grip it between both of mine. "Shit happened, and I'm moving on. You should, too."

His eyes narrow on my face. "We're not talking about me." His expression grows softer. "You killed a man and watched another woman die. You got drugged and beaten.

You don't have to be strong around me. I know it will take time."

God, I love this man.

A smile forms around my lips. "Growing up in Brownsville, I've seen a lot of shit. You learn to accept what happened and go on with your life." Not wanting him to think I'm heartless, I add, "A part of me will always feel sad for Milania, but the rest of the stuff that happened is old news."

He stares at me for a moment, his eyes searching mine. "Okay." He lets out a sigh, then spits out the truth, "I don't want you to work as a janitor."

Letting go of his hand, I cross my arms over my chest. I tilt my head, raising my right eyebrow. "So you are firing me."

"No. Can't you think of it as a promotion?"

"A promotion to what?"

"My personal assistant whose only job is to give me love twenty-four-seven."

I let out a burst of laughter because, even though he's so freaking sweet, he drives me crazy.

"I can't be a stay-at-home wife. I need to keep busy."

He wraps his arms around me. "I like the sound of stay-at-home wife."

"No."

His eyes drift over my face. "I don't want you working nights. I want you next to me in bed where you belong."

Understanding where he's coming from, I say, "Fine, but I still need to find a job for during the day."

"Okay."

"You're not going to fight me on it?"

He shakes his head. "As long as you work regular hours, we're good."

I step closer to him. "You're kind of bossy." I press a kiss to his jaw and give him a seductive look. "I like it."

"Hmm…"

Dario lifts me from my feet, and I wrap my legs around his waist. He carries me to the bedroom and kicks the door shut with his foot.

"Are you trying to distract me from going job hunting?" I ask, my voice filled with lust.

"Yes. I'm going to fuck all the restless energy out of you."

"Are you going to fuck me into submission, Mr. La Rosa?" I tease before my teeth tug at his earlobe.

I'm shoved down on the bed, and like a man possessed, Dario practically rips my jeans and sweater off.

I don't even have time to undo half the buttons on his shirt when he pushes my legs open and aligns his cock with my entrance.

Dario enters me so hard, my body curls forward, and my fingers grip his shirt as if my life depends on it.

"Jesus," I gasp.

He pulls out, and when he slams into me again, a growl ripples from his chest.

Not having time to struggle with buttons, I rip his shirt open so my hands can feast on his chest.

Dario's fingers wrap around my throat. He forces my head back, then his mouth claims mine in a kiss that makes my abdomen tighten and my pussy clench around his cock.

He keeps plunging into me, and needing somewhere to hold onto, I grab hold of his ass. It allows me to feel how his muscles tighten with every thrust, and my ovaries practically explode.

"Shit, Dario," I whimper from how intense it feels. "Baby, I need–"

I'm shoved down onto the bed, his grip around my throat tightening until he's a second away from cutting off my air supply. His other hand grips my hip, and he hammers hard into me.

"Ah," is the only sound I can make as he sets fire to my pussy with his cock.

My body keeps tensing more and more, pleasure threatening to overwhelm me at any moment. It keeps building and building and fucking building until I let out a desperate cry.

Dario's thumb brushes lightly over my clit, and it's all it takes to make me detonate like a bomb.

The orgasm is so intense I can't breathe and lose complete control of my body as it convulses.

"That's right, *Tesoro*. Come hard for me," Dario growls as his pace turns from rough to short, quick thrusts.

Whimpers start to spill over my lips, my eyes locked on his face that looks borderline brutal.

His fingers tighten even more around my neck, and I gasp for air, my hand flying up to grab hold of his wrist.

A second later, he jerks inside me with a groan, and his grip on my neck eases enough for me to breathe.

He keeps fucking me through his orgasm, and each thrust intensifies the pleasure still seizing my body.

Dario's mouth finds mine again, and as his movements slow to a leisurely pace, he kisses me the way he did on our first date.

It feels as if he's worshiping me, and my heart surrenders completely to him.

I let go of the old and embrace this new life that's been given to me.

His arm slips around me, and I'm moved further up the bed before he lies down on top of me, his mouth never leaving mine.

His cock pushes back inside me before he keeps still, showing me how much he loves me with his tongue and teeth.

I'm so caught up in my man, I have no idea how much time passes. At some point, Dario begins moving again, this time keeping the pace slow and deep as he fills me with his cock.

There's a buzz of pleasure that keeps growing in intensity, and it feels like I'm just orgasming and orgasming.

It's heaven, and I don't want this moment between us to end.

Dario frees my swollen lips, and locking eyes with me, he whispers, "I love you so fucking much."

I wrap my arms and legs around him, and cling to him as he finds his release for a second time deep inside me.

While he shudders through his orgasm, I say, "I love you just as much, baby."

When we're completely satisfied and tired, he doesn't move off me, but just keeps staring at me.

Lifting my hand to his hair, I brush my fingers through the light brown strands and ask, "What are you thinking about?"

"That I could stay in this position all night."

"We don't have to get up." My lips curve up. "I love feeling you inside me."

"Good," he murmurs before feathering kisses along my jaw. "*Adoro il modo in cui si sente la tua figa attorno al mio cazzo.*"

Brushing my hands up and down his broad back, I ask, "What does it mean?"

"I love the way your pussy feels around my cock."

Remembering he said those words before, I grin up at him.

Hearing Bella scratch by the door, Dario presses another kiss to my mouth before he climbs off me.

I scoot off the bed, and as I walk to the bathroom, he opens the door slightly so Bella can squeeze through the gap, then shuts it again.

In the mood for a relaxing hot bath, I open the faucets to let water in before I quickly clean between my legs.

"Whatever happened to you getting condoms?" I call out so he'll hear me in the bedroom.

"I think they're in the bedside drawer," he mutters as he comes butt-naked into the bathroom.

I haven't had much of a chance to look at his body, and I let my eyes slowly drift over every inch of him.

Bella makes herself comfortable on the bathroom mat, happy to be near us.

"You're hot," I mention, my gaze still feasting on him.

"Glad you like what you see, *Tesoro*."

When there's enough water in the tub that's probably as big as the bathroom in my apartment, I get in.

"Move up," Dario orders before climbing in behind me.

He pulls me backward until I'm resting against his chest.

Soaking in the warm water, I let out a happy sigh.

"Want me to ask Skylar if she needs another waitress?" he asks.

I move my head so I can glance up at him. "You wouldn't mind?"

"Not at all. I'd prefer it if you worked at *Yukhaejang*."

"I bet the tips there are awesome," I mutter.

"And the hours are reasonable," he adds.

True. It won't take up all my time, which will give me a chance to explore and idea I've been playing with. Now that I have more money than I know what to do with, I want to give something back to the community I grew up in.

I just have to think of a way I can make a difference in their lives.

Chapter 34

Dario

I managed to track down Miguel's uncle and passed the information on to Damiano, who sent his men to capture him.

While we're waiting for them to return, I'm still searching for Miguel, who's somewhere in South America.

"You wanted to see me?" Tyrone asks.

I glance over my shoulder and nod. "Come take a seat."

I wait for him to sit down, his eyes flicking over my system before settling on me.

"I have a job offer for you," I get right to the point.

His eyebrow lifts. "Yeah?"

"How would you feel about driving Eden around and being her bodyguard?"

He doesn't even think about the question. "I'd like to do that. Beats working construction."

"I'll send you for defensive driving courses and weapons training."

This time, his eyebrows fly up. "Okay."

"Ever fired a gun?" I ask as I get up to grab a Glock from the cabinet where I keep all my weapons.

"Yeah. I shot bottles and shit as a teenager."

Letting out a chuckle, I shake my head and sit down again. Taking the magazine out, I reload it and show him the basics before I hand him the gun.

"Just point and shoot," I mutter.

He takes the weapon then locks eyes with me again. "What are we going to do about the drug dealers?"

"Most of them were killed when we searched for Eden," I tell him.

He seems surprised by the news but then says, "Yeah, but as long as that bitch of a mother keeps using, more will come knocking on Eden's door for payment."

With all the shit that went down and helping Eden to adjust to her new life, I didn't even think about her mother.

"Has it happened before?" I ask. "Dealers coming to Eden for money?"

"Yeah, and every time Eden ends up beaten. The shit has to stop."

He's right.

"I'll take care of the problem," I say so he won't worry.

He shifts in the chair. "I can't live here forever. When can I go back to my place?"

"About that..." I suck in a deep breath of air, then say, "If you move back to Brownsville, you'll have to travel up and down at all hours to drive Eden around."

His eyes narrow slightly. "What you getting at?"

"I own another apartment in this building. It's on the same floor as Esmerelda's place. Move in there so you're close to Eden."

Shock tightens his features, and he just stares at me.

I give him a few seconds to recover, then add, "The place is furnished, but you're welcome to bring your own furniture as well."

"How much will the rent be?" he asks.

Fuck.

"Well, I'm going to pay you twenty thousand a month. You don't have to pay rent, but if you insist, we can make it an even two thousand."

"Dafuq?" he mutters, looking at me as if I've grown two heads. "You're gonna pay me twenty thousand? Dollars? A month? Just to drive Eden's ass around town?"

"Yes."

"Man, oh man."

He shoots up from his chair and starts to pace up and down my office as if he's a boxer getting ready to fight.

"Man, bro." He stops to look at me with so much emotion I feel the punch in my heart. "Come here, son."

I'm hauled out of the chair and almost get a rib broken from the tight hug he's giving me.

I pat him on the back. "Tyrone…ribs."

"Sorry." He lets go of me then slaps me on the shoulder. "You sure you wanna do all that for me?"

"Yeah, but I'd prefer if you didn't pay rent. The place is empty anyway."

"No, I gotta pay my way in life. It will feel like I'm doing something to earn my spot in this classy building." He shakes his head again, a look of disbelief still on his face.

"In that case, the rent is due on the last day of the month. You can leave the cash with Esmerelda so she can use it for groceries."

Opening one of the drawers at my desk, I pull a set of keys out and toss them at Tyrone.

He catches them, the smile on his face so wide all I see is a row of white teeth.

Giving me the sincerest expression I've ever seen, he says, "You have a good heart, Dario. Thanks for everything."

"You're welcome."

He gives me a hopeful look. "Can I go look at the apartment?"

"Sure." I get up, and as we leave the office, he hollers, "Baby girl, where you at? Your old man has good news."

"Downstairs," she answers.

When we come down the stairs, he jingles the keys in the air. "Dario just gave me the keys to a fancy-ass apartment in this building."

"What?" she gasps, stopping what she was doing on the laptop. "For real?"

"Yes. I'm gonna pay him rent."

Her eyes meet mine, and she gives me a grateful look before she gets up from the couch and walks closer to us.

"Wanna come with? I'm gonna check out my new crib," Tyrone asks with excitement lacing his words.

"Yeah, we're coming with," Eden answers for both of us.

We all bundle into the elevator, and I press the button for the fifth floor.

On the ride down, Tyrone says, "I also got a new job."

"You did?" Eden asks, glancing up at him. "Doing what?"

"Driving your ass around. I'm gonna be your driver slash bodyguard."

She raises an eyebrow at us. "My driver? For what? I don't have many places to go."

"It's for my peace of mind," I mutter. "And Tyrone's. We only want to keep you safe."

"Aww…"

"It's good pay," Tyrone adds. "So don't get me in trouble with the boss."

"Boss, my ass," I mumble as the doors open.

We walk to the apartment, and when Tyrone unlocks the front door, I notice his hand's shaking a little. He pushes the door open, and stepping inside, he lets out a long whistle.

"Wow. Nicccce," Eden comments.

They glance around, and I can feel the excitement coming in waves off Tyrone. Before I can take cover, he comes at me and yanks me into a bear-hug.

"Thank you," he whispers, sounding choked up. "You don't know how much this means to me. Everything you've done for my girl and me…" He shakes his head as he lets go and wipes over his eyes. "Damn man. It's like we won the lotto."

I pat his arm. "You're welcome."

Eden watches us from the side, her features tight with emotion.

Thinking they might want some time alone, I say, "I'm heading back to my place. You guys stay and look around."

I start to walk toward the door, but Eden catches up to me and presses a kiss to my cheek. "Thank you for doing all of this."

I nod before leaving the apartment so I can get back to work.

On the ride up in the elevator, my thoughts turn to Eden's mom. She's placed my woman's life in danger multiple times with her addiction problem.

When the doors open, I walk through the foyer and head back to my office while pulling out my phone.

Dialing a number, I listen as it rings.

"Frankie speaking."

"It's Dario."

"What can I do for you?"

"I need cocaine."

"Say what?"

"It's not for me dumbass," I snap.

"Oh…ahh…it will take me a couple of hours. Since your boss sent his men into the area, the dealers have been hiding."

"Call me when you have it."

"I need money to get powder," Frankie reminds me.

"I'll make a transfer now."

I end the call and take a seat on the chair by my desk.

I plan on giving Mandy the weapon so she can take herself out. It's the only way to keep Eden safe.

Focusing my attention on my system, I get back to work, searching for Miguel so we can close the chapter on the fucker.

Chapter 35

Eden

Walking into *Yukhaejang*, the restaurant where Dario brought me on our first date, I feel nervous for a different reason.

I glance at the tables and customers, thinking this place is the complete opposite of the diner.

Walking to a stand where a woman is reading something, I wait for her to look at me before I say, "I'm here to see Skylar."

A frown forms on her forehead. "The chef?"

"Yes." Worried I'm going to be kicked out, I add, "She's expecting me."

"Oh."

As the woman glances over her shoulder, I see Skylar coming from the kitchen.

Thank God.

A smile spreads over her face when she notices me. "You're here. Come to the back."

I dart around the stand, and when I reach Skylar, she gives me a quick hug.

"Thanks for agreeing to see me," I say while we walk to an office.

When she shuts the door behind us, she smiles at me again. "Let's get the business out of the way so we can relax."

"Yeah…okay."

She gestures at a chair, and even though I feel too nervous, I sit down.

"Dario says you have experience in waitressing?"

"Yes. I worked at Ben's Burgers since I was sixteen."

"He mentioned the diner. Did you do anything else, or just waitressing?"

"I've cashed up at closing time, helped with schedules, and placed and received orders. You know, the usual stuff that goes on in a diner."

She stares at me for a moment, which doesn't help my nerves shit, then she says, "I have a manager's assistant position open. You'll have to help keep the fridge stocked and plan the serving staff schedule."

"Really?" I gasp. "That would be awesome."

Skylar lets out a chuckle. "I have one rule, though."

"What?"

"If we butt heads at work, it can't affect our personal relationship."

"Personal relationship?" I parrot her.

"We're going to become friends, Eden. Dario and Renzo are close, and we'll spend a lot of time together outside of work."

"Oh, right. Sorry," I chuckle. "I forgot about that."

She reaches her hand out to me, and when I shake it, she says, "Welcome to the team."

"Thank you so much." I feel some of the tension leave my body. "When do you want me to start?"

"The second week of January."

"That's still a month away," I mention. "You sure?"

"A certain person wants to spend the holidays with you before I steal all your time."

Laughter bursts from me. "Dario?"

"Yes."

With the business out of the way, she asks, "How are you doing after...?" She lets the sentence trail away, but I know what she's referring to.

"Much better. I'm back to my old self."

"Did Dario mention we all get together once a month?"

I shake my head.

"It's Tori and Angelo's turn this month. It was Renzo's and mine last month, and we had Thanksgiving here at the restaurant."

"You all sound really close," I mention.

"We are." Her eyes lock with mine. "You'll get used to it." She stands up. "Remind Dario about the dinner at Tori and Angelo's place on Christmas Eve. Oh, before I forget, we can arrange for you to come in a week before you're due to start so you can meet all the staff and explain the job in more detail and talk about your pay. Will you be okay with that?"

"Yes, that would be great," I murmur as I get up and follow her out of the office.

"Sorry, I can't talk longer, but I need to get back to the kitchen."

"Oh, sure. I totally understand."

She gives me another quick hug before rushing back to work.

When I walk out of the restaurant, it's to see Tyrone leaning against the SUV with sunglasses on.

I can't help but start laughing, which has his head turning in my direction.

"I look cool, don't I?" he asks.

"Yeah, totally badass."

He opens the front passenger door for me. "Seat belt, baby girl."

"Yes, Dad," I tease him.

Tyrone freezes, then his features tighten with emotion. "I like the sound of that."

Jesus. My heart.

He shuts the door, and walking around the front of the SUV, he slides in behind the steering wheel.

As he starts the engine and drives down the street, I ask, "Would it be okay if I called you Dad?"

He clears his throat. "I'd love it."

We're quiet again, then he asks, "Where to?"

"The diner."

The ride to Brownsville is filled with emotion, and Tyrone keeps clearing his throat while I blink my ass off to keep the tears back.

When he pulls up to Ben's Burgers and places the car in park, I lean over and kiss his cheek. "Thank you for being my father."

I shove the door open and quickly climb out.

When Tyrone…Dad joins me, he mutters, "I swear you want to see your old man weep like a baby."

As soon as we walk into the diner, Sherrie lets out a shriek and comes to hug me.

"I thought you forgot about us."

"Never," I chuckle.

She gestures at the SUV. "Who's ride is that?"

"Mine," Dad mutters before he finds an open seat.

"For real?" Sherrie asks.

"Yeah," I reply. "I have a lot to tell you."

"Can I get a refill," Jovan, one of the regulars, asks.

"Give me a minute," she tells him before turning her attention back to me.

"Give him a refill. I'll talk while you work," I say so she won't get in trouble with Sylvia.

She grabs the coffee pot and as we walk from table to table, I tell her everything that's happened the past two to three weeks.

By the time I'm done, she's staring at me with wide eyes, the coffee pot forgotten in her hand.

"Damn, girl. Besides the shit with the drug dealers, you're living the fairy-tale life the rest of us dream about." She gives me a playful punch on the shoulder. "Good for you."

"Right?" I grin from ear to ear, then do something I've always wanted to do, and shout, "Pie's on me, people!"

I haven't spent a dime of the money Dario gave me and figured this is the best way to start.

The customers cheer, and I get to work, helping Sherrie serve everyone a slice of pie.

When I take a seat by Dad to wait while he eats his slice, I say, "I'm going to miss this place."

"You spent a lot of time here."

"Yeah."

"On to bigger and better things," he murmurs before washing the pie down with a sip of coffee.

"Talking about bigger and better. Want to open a soup kitchen with me?"

"Here in Brownsville?"

I nod. "I was thinking we can talk to the church and get something going."

"Is that really how you wanna spend the money Dario gave you?"

I mentioned the money to him during the drive to the restaurant but didn't tell him how much. I'm still trying to process the amount, so it will probably give Dad a heart attack, which is the last thing I want.

Answering his question, I say, "Yes. I want to give back to the community."

"We can stop at the church over on Riverdale Avenue before we head home."

"Thanks."

Leaning back in my seat I glance around the diner, thinking how much my life has changed.

One moment, I'm a struggling waitress slash janitor, and the next, I'm dating Dario La Rosa, mafia boss slash art lover.

How the hell did I get this lucky?

Chapter 36

Dario

I've just picked up the drugs from Frankie, and driving up a street in Brownsville, I recognize an SUV parked outside of a diner.

I slow down, and when I park behind the vehicle, I see Eden and Tyrone sitting in a booth. It looks like they're eating pie.

I push the R8's door open to get out, but an alarm on my phone has me digging the device out.

Seeing an alert regarding Miguel, I quickly go into the app. He's been spotted in Miami.

Christ. We have to move fast.

I shut the door again, and starting the engine, I pull away from the curb while dialing Damiano's number.

"You better have good news for me. My men killed the fucking uncle," he mutters.

"Miguel's in Miami," I say, feeling good that I finally get to give him solid information.

"Wheels up in thirty minutes," he grumbles. "Let the others know we're meeting at the airfield."

"On it."

The call ends and when I stop at a traffic light, I quickly send a group text out.

Miguel spotted in Miami. Meet at the airfield stat. Wheels up in 30.

The light turns green as I dial Eden's number, and driving out of Brownsville, I listen to the call ring.

"Hey," she answers.

"I'm heading out of town for business. I don't know how long it will take."

"What kind of business?" she asks.

"Cosa Nostra. We're going after Miguel," I answer honestly, not wanting to keep her in the dark regarding this side of my life.

Her tone is tense with worry when she asks, "Will it be dangerous?"

"I'll be fine, *Tesoro*. You don't have to worry when I'm taking care of mafia business."

"Easier said than done," she mutters. "Will you be able to call me while you're working?"

"Yes. I'll check in on you every couple of hours. Don't worry, and enjoy your pie."

"Pie?" she mumbles, then her voice pitches as she exclaims, "How did you know I'm having pie?!"

"I'm always watching you," I chuckle.

"Hmm…I like knowing I have a hot stalker," she teases me.

Another call beeps, and it has me saying, "I have to go. Love you, *Tesoro*."

"Love you too, baby."

Hearing those words from her has a wide smile stretching over my face.

I end the call and answer the other one. "Dario."

"Where are you?" Franco asks.

"On my way to the airfield."

"I can't join you on this trip, and Damiano's not answering his goddamn phone. The triplets have the shits. Sam and I are running on zero sleep."

"I'll tell him."

"Thanks. Be careful out there."

"Okay. Good luck, and I hope the babies feel better soon."

"From your lips to God's ears," he mutters before hanging up.

I try Damiano's number but it's engaged.

At another set of traffic lights, I send Esmerelda a text.

Going to Miami for work. Take care of Eden and Bella for me.

The lights change to green, and it takes me another twenty minutes to get to the airfield.

"Thirty minutes, my fucking ass," I mumble as I stop the R8 near the private jet.

I'm first, and that's only because I was already driving.

I don't have to wait long, though. Renzo arrives second with Vincenzo and Fabrizio, then Angelo and Big Ricky.

We all stand near the plane when three SUVs come driving toward us before stopping with screeching tires.

Damiano climbs out, muttering something under his breath while looking like he's about to rip someone's head off.

"It's a good day," I say. "We know where Miguel is. Why aren't you happy?"

"I am."

"Sure as fuck doesn't look like it."

"Dario, I'm not in the mood for your shit today. Let's get this over with so I can take some time off to deal with–"

He stops talking which has all of us raising eyebrows at him.

"Get on the fucking plane," he shouts.

Curious as fuck, I bite my tongue and board the private jet.

As the pilots prepare for take-off, I grab a seat next to Renzo while Angelo takes the one beside Damiano. The rest of the men grab an open seat and wisely keep the noise level down, seeing as Damiano is in one hell of a mood.

"Franco's babies are sick," I tell our boss. "They all have the shits."

"Christ, poor man," Angelo mutters. "I'd rather go to war than deal with three babies who all have diarrhea."

"Can we not talk about shit," Damiano growls.

"Seriously, who pissed you off?" Angelo asks him.

"Just focus on the mission," he snaps.

As soon as we're in the air, I get up and retrieve the bag of weapons we keep on board from the compartment.

I check my rifle and scope while the others do the same with their weapons. When I'm satisfied that the rifle is ready, I place it back in the shoulder bag.

Settling into my seat again, I pull out my phone and go into my app so I can check whether Miguel's been spotted anywhere else.

An hour later, I let out a sigh because there's been no other sightings of the man.

"What?" Renzo asks.

"Miguel hasn't been spotted again."

"Where was he last seen?" Damiano asks, his eyes trained on the oval window beside him.

"A set of traffic lights near one of his clubs," I answer.

"He'll probably be there until late," Renzo mutters. "Which means we'll have to wait him out."

"Or we go in." Damiano turns his gaze to us. "I want this done as quickly as possible. We've wasted enough time on this fucker."

I agree.

"How do you want to do this, Damiano?" Angelo asks.

He thinks for a moment, then says, "We'll all go into the club. Our men, as well." Pausing, he rubs his fingers over the scruff on his jaw. "We'll walk up to the fucker as a family, and I'll kill him in front of everyone. It will send a message not to fuck with us."

"And the witnesses?" Renzo asks.

"Let them talk."

I let out a sigh because that means we're going to have to call in favors and bribe lots of officials to keep Damiano's ass out of prison.

But what he wants, he gets, so none of us argue.

When the convoy of SUVs pulls up to the club, I glance around the area.

It's quiet outside the club because it's early and the place isn't open yet.

"What do you want to do?" Renzo asks Damiano.

"Let's go knock on the door," he mutters, shoving the car door open.

"You think they're just going to open for us?" Renzo asks as we all climb out of the SUV.

"Of course not," Damiano growls, giving Renzo a what the fuck look. "I'm not fucking stupid." Lifting his arm, he signals for his men to come.

When I see the grenade launcher, I shake my head. Everyone's going to hear the explosion.

Angelo and I glance at each other, and I can see he's worried about Damiano. Even for our boss, who's done some crazy shit, this is a little reckless.

"Blow the door," Damiano orders.

Leaving my rifle in the car because I sure as shit won't need it in a club, I pull one of my Heckler & Kochs from behind my back, where it's tucked into my waistband.

Renzo and Angelo also hold their guns ready.

The grenade blows a hole in the front of the club, and I suck in a deep breath of air before I follow my friends over the rubble and into a dark hallway.

Smoke hangs in the air, and I duck my head low, trying to avoid inhaling it.

As soon as we reach an open space with a dance floor and bars, the fuckers open fire on us.

Renzo and I duck to the side and run toward a bar, where we take cover. I have no idea where Angelo and Damiano went.

Renzo shakes his head and mutters, "Damiano seriously needs to get laid. It will do wonders for his temper." He darts up, takes a quick look, then crouches in front of me again. "Cover me. I'm going to make a run for the DJ's booth."

He darts out from behind the bar, and I shoot up and open fire on the fuckers that are on the second floor while mumbling, "Who the fuck's going to cover me?"

I watch as a bullet clips Renzo's arm just as he ducks behind the booth and take out the fucker who shot my friend before I make a run for it.

Don't get yourself killed today, Dario.

Chapter 37

Dario

I feel a stinging sensation across my side as a bullet narrowly misses me before I fall and slide straight into Renzo.

"Christ," he grunts. "You okay?"

"Yeah." I check the magazine in my gun, then I slam it back into place. "We should've brought machine guns," I mutter as I move into a crouching position.

"You're bleeding," Renzo says, pulling the fabric of my shirt away from my side.

"So are you. One grazed me. How's your arm?"

"The bullet didn't go deep. I'll live."

"You better."

"Where the fuck are you?" Damiano shouts over the gunfire.

"DJ's booth," Renzo yells.

The gunfire stops suddenly, and we hear our boss bark, "Get your asses out here."

We dart up, and as we leave our cover, it's to see Damiano and Carlo moving up the stairs with Angelo and Big Ricky behind them.

"You watch our backs while I keep an eye on the second floor," I tell Renzo before we run to catch up to the others with Vincenzo and Fabrizio following after us.

Everything is eerily quiet as we take the stairs up, and when we reach the VIP area, Miguel's sitting at a table with his men forming a half circle around him.

"Did you really have to go to all this trouble?" Miguel asks as he stares at Damiano.

"Yes."

Not giving a shit, Damiano pulls out a chair and takes a seat at the table. He gestures for Carlo to pour him a drink.

I move closer while I pull my other Heckler & Koch from behind my back. On guard, my eyes flick from one fucker to the next.

Damiano lets out a sigh. "All you had to do was listen, but no, you had to be stubborn and come into our territory."

"There's a lot of money to be made in New York. The deal still stands," Miguel says, looking a little uneasy.

Carlo places a tumbler of whiskey in front of Damiano, who picks up the drink and takes a sip.

When he sets the tumbler down again, he murmurs, "As good as a thirty percent share sounds, I have to decline."

My heartbeat speeds up again because I recognize the look on his face.

A second later, his arm flies up, and he takes the kill shot, hitting Miguel right between the eyes.

All hell breaks loose, and the rest of us open fire.

A bullet whistles past my head, and I have to drop my empty Heckler & Koch before tackling Damiano off the chair when a fucker has a clear shot of him.

There's another sting across my back before we plow into the floor, with Damiano cushioning my fall.

My arm swings through the air as I spin around, ready for action, but the last man goes down from Big Ricky's bullet.

Slumping back on the carpet, I stare up at the ceiling as I suck in desperate breaths. "Christ."

Still lying beside me, Damiano lifts his hand and holds his thumb and pointer finger an inch apart. "You came this close to kneeing me in the balls, fucker."

I let out a burst of laughter. "I'm pretty sure I took a bullet for you."

"What?" He sits up and starts checking me for wounds.

"Flesh wound on my back."

He shoves at me before climbing to his feet. "That's not taking a fucking bullet." He glances around the area then asks, "Everyone okay?"

"Yeah, just need to visit the clinic," Vincenzo mutters. "I took a bullet in the leg."

Fabrizio moves closer to his friend to help him down the stairs.

"Let's go," Damiano orders.

"Someone going to give me a hand?" I ask.

My boss pauses, then grabs hold of my hand and hauls me to my feet.

I glance at Miguel's body but know his death won't stop the drugs from coming into New York. It's a war we'll fight until our dying day.

As soon as we land, I head home to swap the R8 for my SUV before driving toward Brownsville with the bag of cocaine in my pocket.

I'm fucking tired and just want to get into bed with my woman, but first, I have to take care of her mother.

I dial Frankie's number when I reach the neighborhood.

"I'm starting to feel special," he answers.

I let out a chuckle, then ask, "Do you know where Eden's mother hangs out?"

"A bar up the road from the apartment building Eden stayed in."

I need to check whether Eden and Tyrone have given up their leases for the apartments.

"Meet me at the bar."

I end the call and drive to the apartment. Passing by Eden's old building, I see a group of homeless people gathering around a fire they've made in a trashcan.

When I reach a bar, I park the SUV and get out, glancing around for Frankie's sedan.

I don't have to wait long until he comes driving up the road, and as soon as the car stops, he climbs out of the passenger seat.

"What's up?"

"Find Mandy. I need to talk to her."

"Let me check inside."

I watch as he jogs across the road and goes into the bar. Not even a minute later, he hauls a woman out onto the sidewalk, and gripping her arm tightly, he drags her to where I'm standing.

"Thanks, Frankie. You can go," I say as my eyes drift over her.

She looks like she's in her sixties, skinny as fuck, and drunk.

Giving me a smile, she slurs, "Ten bucks for a blow."

I suck in a deep breath before exhaling it slowly, and wanting to give her a chance to save herself, I say, "I'm here to give you a choice. Come with me, and I'll take you to rehab right now. Once you're clean, I'll help you get a job so you can get off the streets."

She lets out a bitter chuckle. "Nah, man, that sounds like too much work. You want a blowie or not?"

Taking the bag of cocaine out of my pocket, I hold it out to her. "Or you can take this."

"What's the catch?" she asks, her eyes latching onto the bag as if it's the holy grail.

"No catch. I just want to give you something for the holidays."

"Thanks." Taking the bag, she doesn't even check for traffic before she crosses the road and disappears down an alley.

Freezing my ass off, I climb back into the SUV to wait for thirty minutes because I need to make sure Mandy won't be a problem for Eden in the future.

My phone vibrates, and I check the message that just came through.

Eden: Just checking if you're okay.

I quickly take off my gloves and type a response.

Dario: Almost done. I'll be home in an hour.

Eden: Can't wait. I have something exciting to share with you.

She probably wants to tell me she's starting to work with Skylar in January.

Putting the gloves on again, the wounds on my arm and back sting, and I know Eden's going to lose her shit when she sees I've been grazed by bullets.

I keep an eye on the time, and when thirty minutes is up, I get out of the SUV and walk to the alley, where I pass empty crates and boxes.

When I see a pair of feet sticking out behind a dumpster, my pace slows. Mandy comes into view, the open bag of cocaine clutched in her hand, her eyes frozen in death while the blood from her nose dries.

It could've been a very different story had she taken the other option.

Turning around, I walk back to the SUV so I can get my ass home to my woman with the full intention of not telling her about Mandy's death. I feel it will be better if Eden learns about it by herself, and if she never finds out, then that's good with me, too.

I climb back into my vehicle, and starting the engine, I drive home while thinking about how my life's changed since I met Eden.

She's in every beat of my heart and every breath I take.

Chapter 38

Eden

When Dario walks into the bedroom looking like hell, I shoot up and rush to his side.

"What the hell happened to you?" When I get a good look at him and notice blood on his shirt, I gasp, "Jesus, Dario! Did you get shot?"

"No." He grips my chin with his fingers, and I smell gunpowder. Locking eyes with me, he says, "I'm fine. Two bullets grazed me. It's nothing serious."

"Let me look at you," I mutter as I yank my chin free and start to unbutton his shirt.

He lets me tug the fabric off, and I exhale a breath of relief when I see the grazed skin on his side.

"You're so damn lucky there's no bullet," I snap as I shoot him a glare. "I swear to God, if you ever die on me, I'm bringing you back so I can kill you myself."

"One grazed me on my back as well," he says as if it's something to be proud of.

"What?!" I dart behind him, and seeing the red welt across his back, I slap him against the shoulder. "Get your ass in the bathroom so I can clean the wounds."

"Scrapes," he corrects me.

I glare at him, and noticing the grin on his face, I shake my head. "What the hell are you smiling about?"

"You." He takes hold of my hip and pulls me closer. "I love how you're fussing over me."

"I'm not fussing over you. I'm fighting with you."

"Fussing..." He kisses my left cheek. "Fighting..." Another kiss on my right cheek. "Same thing." When he leans in to kiss me on the mouth, I pull away and walk into the bathroom.

"*Tesoro*," He chuckles as he follows after me, "I'm fine. Don't be mad at me."

"Have you heard of a bulletproof vest?" I ask as I dig the first aid kit out of the cabinet beneath the sink.

"We forgot."

I shoot another glare his way as I open the kit and take out the antiseptic wipes. "Come here."

He moves closer, and without any warning, I slap the antiseptic wipe against his side.

When he jerks away, I mutter, "It wouldn't hurt right now if you'd been wearing a bulletproof vest. Stand still."

This time around, I work much gentler as I clean the grazed skin on his side and back.

"I love you," he whispers.

"Telling me you love me won't get you out of trouble," I mumble as I clean the abrasions.

"You going to spank me?" he asks with a teasing tone.

"It sure as hell won't be kinky."

When I'm done, I dispose of the wipes and wash my hands before turning to face him again.

Framing his jaw with my palms, I stand on my tiptoes and press a kiss to his mouth. "Promise me you'll be more careful and always wear a bulletproof vest."

"I promise."

When I pull away, he opens the faucets in the shower and starts to undress while mentioning, "You said you had exciting news?"

"Oh, right!" I hop onto the counter next to the sink and take a seat. "I got an assistant manager position at the restaurant. Skylar was so nice. I can't wait to work there."

He gives me a quick kiss, then says, "Congratulations, *Tesoro*."

"Aaaand…" Excitement bubbles in my chest.

He steps beneath the spray and lets the water rush over his body, then asks, "There's more news?"

"Yes. I've decided to open a soup kitchen." I clap my hands together.

Dario turns to face me, lifting an eyebrow while washing his body. "A soup kitchen?"

"Tyrone, who, by the way, I'm calling Dad now, said he'd help me. We stopped by a church, and the pastor was super positive about the idea. He could organize volunteers to help."

I suck in a breath of air, but before I can continue, he says, "Damn, you were busy while I was at work."

I swing my legs back and forth, a happy smile on my face. "I want to put some of the money you gave me to good use. Give back to my community."

"Let me know if you need more funds to get the business up and running. I'm sure all the guys would love to donate to a good cause."

"You think so?"

He nods as he closes the faucets and grabs a towel to dry himself.

"I have a list of things to do. I need to find cooks, and a supplier for food, and I'll probably have to buy a ton of plates and utensils."

Dario presses another kiss to my mouth to silence me, then mentions, "We can hire a team to help you with all the work."

I wrap my arms around his neck and stare at him with all the love I feel. "Thank you." I lock my legs around his waist and pull him closer. "You don't think my idea to open a soup kitchen is stupid or too big a project to take on?"

"No." Picking me up, he carries me to the bed and lays me down on my side of the mattress while continuing, "I think it's an amazing idea. I just don't want you working yourself to death."

"Okay."

Walking around the bed, he throws the covers back and lies down beside me. I crawl beneath the blankets and adjust them over his body before I get comfortable.

He turns so we're lying face-to-face, then says, "You're one hell of an amazing woman, Eden."

I brush my fingers over the five o'clock shadow on his jaw. "You're even more amazing."

We're quiet for a moment, just staring at each other, then I say, "Remember when I said I was worried we'd break up and I wouldn't have anywhere to go? I'm not worried anymore. I know we're going to make it as a couple."

"Yeah? What made you change your mind?"

"You," I whisper. "You've gone above and beyond for me and Tyrone, and seeing how kind and caring you are made me realize I can trust you not to break my heart."

He shifts a little closer until there's only an inch between our faces. "I love you with all of my heart, *Tesoro*."

"I love you too, baby."

We continue to stare at each other until he drifts off to sleep. Careful not to wake him, I leave the room to switch off all the lights in the apartment. I grab Bella from where she was sleeping on the couch and head back up the stairs.

Heading to the bedroom, I climb into bed again and wait for Bella to find a comfortable position by my feet before I scoot as close as I can to Dario without waking him.

I take a deep breath of his scent and when my sight adjusts to the dark, and I can see him a little clearer, I keep staring at his handsome face as I grow sleepy.

I don't know what I did to deserve this man but thank you.

I send the prayer out into the universe, and with a heart filled with love and happiness, I fall asleep.

Epilogue

Eden

(One year later…)

My life has been a whirlwind of excitement, happiness, love, and hard work.

Emphasis on the hard work.

The soup kitchen has taken up so much of my time this past year, I'm surprised Dario hasn't lost his shit yet.

The man is a saint.

It's the one-year anniversary of when I first opened the soup kitchen's doors to the community, and I now have a team of over twenty people working for me.

I had to give up the assistant manager position at Skylar's restaurant, but luckily she understood. I think it was for the best because we've grown closer as friends, and I would hate for work to get in the way of our friendship.

"Jesus," Sherrie gasps as she stares at all the food containers being carried in by a catering company. "It looks like we're feeding an army."

I let out a chuckle. "We are. Back to work."

Sherrie's been helping out whenever she can, and I always make it worth her time.

We continue setting up the coffee and pie section, and when we're done, I head to the other side of the hall to make sure the food's right.

The catering company was Dario's idea. He also paid a hell of a lot of money to foot the bill.

"Eden, stop doing all the work and let the staff handle it," Sherrie says. "Dario asked you to meet him out front."

"I don't have time! The doors are going to open at any moment."

"Then you better hurry."

Letting out a sigh, I rush to the exit, and the moment I walk outside, surprise brings me to a sudden stop.

There's a huge crowd of people filling the parking area, all here to celebrate the successful year we've had. In the middle of the crowd is a small stage decorated with twinkling lights and flowers.

Dario takes the steps up to the stage then speaks into a microphone. "Can the beautiful lady right at the back please come forward so I don't look like an idiot in front of all these people?"

Jesus.

As I begin to walk, the crowd parts for me, and wherever I look, I see a familiar face.

Emotion wells in my chest, and I have to fight not to cry, but when I see our friends and Dad standing at the foot of the stairs, I can't stop the tears from rolling down my cheeks.

I take the steps up to Dario, who's giving me a loving smile.

"Hi," I whisper. "What are we doing up here?"

"Louder for the people in the back," Dad shouts.

Dario keeps the microphone between us as he says, "The first time I saw you dance, you captured me under your spell, and not a day has passed where I haven't fallen more and more in love with you."

My breathing speeds up, along with my heartbeat, and I wipe my palms on the fabric of my dress.

Dario goes down on one knee, and looking up at me, he continues, "I want to spend my life under your spell, Eden, and the only way I can think of making sure that happens is by begging you to marry me."

A sob bursts from me, and I sink to my knees so we're face-to-face as he asks, "Will you do me the honor of becoming my wife?"

"Yes," I croak, too emotional to speak any louder.

I shove the microphone out of the way and throw my arms around his neck, whispering, "Yes, I'll marry you, Dario. Yes, a million times yes."

He presses a kiss to my lips before pushing me back so he can slip a diamond the size of Texas onto my ring finger.

"Thank you, *Tesoro*, for making me the happiest man alive."

Holding him as tight as I can, I say, "Not half as happy as you've made me."

"Let's get everyone fed," Dad calls out.

As the people head into the hall, I stare at Dario, who took one look at me and decided I was his, and now I'm wearing his ring.

God, I'm so lucky he caught me dancing.

The End.

Published Books
In Reading Order:

MAFIA ROMANCE

THE KINGS OF MAFIA SERIES
Mafia / Organized Crime / Suspense Romance
(Can be read in this order or as standalones)
This series is not connected to any other series I've written, and there will be no spin-offs.

Tempted By The Devil
Craving Danger
Hunted By A Shadow
Drawn To Darkness
Coming 26th Aug 2024…
God Of Vengeance

(The Saints, Sinners & Corrupted Royals all take place in the same world)

THE SAINTS SERIES
Mafia / Organized Crime / Suspense Romance
(Can be read in this order or as standalones)

Merciless Saints

Cruel Saints
Ruthless Saints
Tears of Betrayal
Tears of Salvation

THE SINNERS SERIES
Mafia / Organized Crime / Suspense Romance
(Can be read in this order or as standalones)

Taken By A Sinner
Owned By A Sinner
Stolen By A Sinner
Chosen By A Sinner
Captured By A Sinner

CORRUPTED ROYALS
Mafia / Organized Crime / Suspense Romance
(Can be read in this order or as standalones)

Destroy Me
Control Me
Brutalize Me
Restrain Me
Possess Me

CONTEMPORARY ROMANCE

BEAUTIFULLY BROKEN SERIES

Organized Crime / Suspense Romance
(Can be read in this order or as standalones)

Beautifully Broken
Beautifully Hurt
Beautifully Destroyed

ENEMIES TO LOVERS

College Romance / New Adult / Billionaire Romance

Heartless
Reckless
Careless
Ruthless
Shameless

TRINITY ACADEMY

College Romance / New Adult / Billionaire Romance

Falcon
Mason
Lake
Julian

The Epilogue

THE HEIRS

College Romance / New Adult / Billionaire Romance

Coldhearted Heir
Arrogant Heir
Defiant Heir
Loyal Heir
Callous Heir
Sinful Heir
Tempted Heir
Forbidden Heir

Stand Alone Spin-off
Not My Hero
Young Adult / High School Romance

THE SOUTHERN HEROES SERIES

Suspense Romance / Contemporary Romance / Police Officers & Detectives

The Ocean Between Us
The Girl In The Closet
The Lies We Tell Ourselves
All The Wasted Time
We Were Lost

STANDALONES

<u>LIFELINE</u>
(FBI Suspense Romance)

<u>UNFORGETTABLE</u>
Co-written with Tayla Louise
(Contemporary/Billionaire Romance)

Connect with me

Newsletter

FaceBook

Amazon

GoodReads

BookBub

Instagram

Acknowledgments

After an amazing vacation I'm back with Dario and Eden's story. I just want to thank my readers for being patient during my time away and welcoming me back so warmly.

To Sheldon for all the help with graphics, formatting, and research. Without him, I'd be a mess, and there would be no books.

To Tayla for being my sanity and biggest cheerleader.

My editor, Sheena, has nerves of steel with all the deadlines wooshing past us. Thank you for putting up with me and always being honest with your feedback. I appreciate you so much!

To my alpha and beta readers – Leeann, Brittney, Sherrie, and Sarah thank you for being the godparents of my paper-baby. Thank you for all your time and feedback.

Candi Kane PR - Thank you for being patient with me and my bad habit of missing deadlines. Thank you for being my friend and always being there to calm me down.

Sarah, from *Okay Creations* – I love, love, love the Kings of Mafia covers! Thank you for doing such an amazing job with them.

My street team, thank you for promoting my books. It means the world to me!

A special thank you to every blogger and reader who took the time to participate in the cover reveal and release day.

Love,

Michelle.

Made in the USA
Monee, IL
21 July 2024

62441881R00207